PENGUIN ARCHIVE

Secretary

Mary Gaitskill
b. 1954
A PENGUIN SINCE 2019

Mary Gaitskill
Secretary

PENGUIN ARCHIVE

PENGUIN BOOKS

UK | USA | Canada | Ireland | Australia
India | New Zealand | South Africa

Penguin Books is part of the Penguin Random House group of companies
whose addresses can be found at global.penguinrandomhouse.com.

Penguin Random House UK,
One Embassy Gardens, 8 Viaduct Gardens, London SW11 7BW

penguin.co.uk

'Trying to Be' and 'Secretary' from *Bad Behavior*, first published
in the United States by Simon and Schuster Inc. 1988
'The Dentist' and 'Because They Wanted To' from *Because They Wanted To*,
first published in the United States by Simon and Schuster Inc. 1997
This selection published in Penguin Classics 2025
001

Copyright © Mary Gaitskill, 1988, 1997

No part of this book may be used or reproduced in any manner for the
purpose of training artificial intelligence technologies or systems. In accordance
with Article 4(3) of the DSM Directive 2019/790, Penguin Random House
expressly reserves this work from the text and data mining exception.

Set in 10.25/12.75pt Dante MT Std
Typeset by Jouve (UK), Milton Keynes
Printed and bound in Great Britain by Clays Ltd, Elcograf S.p.A.

The authorized representative in the EEA is Penguin Random House Ireland,
Morrison Chambers, 32 Nassau Street, Dublin D02 YH68

A CIP catalogue record for this book is available from the British Library

ISBN: 978–0–241–75221–0

Penguin Random House is committed to a sustainable future
for our business, our readers and our planet. This book is made from
Forest Stewardship Council® certified paper.

Contents

Trying to Be	1
The Dentist	31
Secretary	72
Because They Wanted To	91

Trying to Be

Stephanie wasn't a 'professional lady' exactly; tricking was just something she slipped into, once a year or so, when she was feeling particularly revolted by clerical work, or when she couldn't pay her bills. She even liked a few of her customers, but she had never considered dating one; she kept her secret forays into prostitution neatly boxed and stored away from her real life. She was thus a little dismayed to find herself standing in high heels and underwear in front of the smeared mirror in the 'Shadow Room,' handing her phone number to Bernard the lawyer. She felt she was being drawn deeper into something she had no business doing in the first place, but she had no boyfriend, she liked the lawyer and, since he was married, it seemed likely he would leave only a faint impression on her life.

She had been working at her current 'house' for three nights when she met him. It wasn't as posh or expensive as the other two places she'd worked, but it was comfortable and safe. She hadn't wanted to go back to the first place because of the peculiarity of the manager, who'd read the girls' auras daily and made them chant over anointed candles in the kitchen to 'purify the space'; and she couldn't go back to the second because it had been closed by the Mafia. She wasn't well connected or knowledgeable enough to systematically search for the best establishment, so she had settled for this – a run-down townhouse apartment with poor ventilation and sad old smells coiling through the rooms. It was called 'Christine's' after the woman who ran it, a tiny frantic blond tyrant who rather desperately fancied her hideous paisley sitting room to be a salon and forced long minutes of excruciating conversation between women and johns before allowing them to escape up the stairs. 'We're known for our intellectual women,' she told Stephanie during her interview. 'Everybody here does something. Alana here is an artist. Suzie is a fashion designer and Beatrice is a nurse.' The three women on the couch regarded Stephanie blankly. Christine gave Stephanie the working name 'Perry' and told her to wear something in which she could 'meet her mother for lunch and then rendezvous with her boyfriend for cocktails.' This ridiculous pretense, teetering pathetically toward aspiration, appealed to her. She thought: It's only for a few weeks, and showed up two days later in a tight silver minidress.

She had come downstairs, after being summoned through the intercom to 'meet someone,' hurried and disheveled, one stocking badly run, having left her portly, huffing client to finish his ablutions alone. She stood before the new man, feeling slightly knock-kneed in her short black skirt, smiling goofily and thinking, for some reason, of the *I Love Lucy* show. The canned laughter mumbled as Christine folded her hands and asked, 'Well, Bernard, would you like to see Perry?'

The man stood up and said, 'Yes, very much.' He was about forty-five, very tall and thin, and wore an absurd bow tie with his conservative suit. He had kind eyes and an intelligent, inquisitive demeanor. She felt that something about her genuinely excited him, and she was flattered.

He followed her to the awful burgundy Shadow Room. He stripped and lay on the bed, his torso resting against a pillow, his slender naked body placidly expectant, his almost alarmingly large penis lying half-hard on his thigh. She took off her

Trying to Be

high heels and knelt beside him on the bed. He didn't touch her or even move closer, he just lay there and looked at her as though he were waiting to be amused. The old air conditioner moaned and dripped.

'I like your hair,' he said. 'It's a becoming style.'

She self-consciously ruffled her spiky, black-dyed crew cut. 'Oh, it's fashionable now. Lots of women have this cut.'

'Yes, I know. But it suits you especially well.'

She said thank you and pulled her shirt over her head.

He glanced at her breasts with apparent approval but still made no move to touch her.

She decided with some relief that he was a talker and settled into conversation.

She quickly found out that he worked for the city on the redevelopment of the Lower East Side, that he did not love his wife, though he was very fond of her, and that they rarely made love. He stayed with her because he didn't want to be alone.

'And what about you? What do you do when you're not at this place?'

She grimaced. 'Well, I don't know if I do anything. I'm trying to become a writer. That's why I came to New York.' She paused, wondering if that sounded ridiculous to this man who wore suits and patronized prostitutes. 'Do you think that's stupid?'

'No, not at all. Why would I think it's stupid?'

'Because so many girls in these houses have the desire to do something else, but it's obvious that in most cases they don't have any talent or are too scared, and I don't know, it just seems sort of pathetic to me. I don't even tell people here what I do. I say I'm a secretary or a dental technical or something.'

'But that's silly. As it happens, I know there have been some very talented people working here. There was a whole coterie of various artists at one point. One of them was a performance artist who went off to Italy and started working with, oh, some avant-garde choreographer – I know the name but I can't think of it. Anyway, I hear she's doing fine.'

'How do you know?'

'I was a regular of hers, and we saw each other on the outside. She had short hair like yours, only hers was orange.' He smiled, as though this disclosed a revealing element that firmly established a relationship between Stephanie and the orange-haired girl. 'As a matter of fact, she used this place to collect material for her work. She was extremely bright and very aware of all the contradictions she embodied by being here.' He smiled gently. 'She could talk about it endlessly.'

She pulled off her skirt and lay down next to him, supporting herself on one elbow. They talked about fiction in *The New Yorker* and *The Atlantic*. She ranted against the trendy writers she despised. They talked about dance performances they'd seen. He described a piece at the Dance Theater Workshop in which the dancers waved large Styrofoam animals at each other and rolled around in paint. She thought it sounded idiotic, but felt tender toward his robustly curious delight in this goofy spectacle.

'I have a Workshop membership and every now and then I get invited to fabulous parties, where all the boys wear long coats and earrings, and all the girls have hair like yours.' He beamed.

She thought: At this rate, I'm not going to have to do anything.

They talked about her past, her coldly perfect father, her sad, passive mother, her sister on lithium, her college major,

Trying to Be

her first romance. He listened gravely. He began to stroke her arm hairs, and then her arm.

He had a seductive touch; she moved closer to him and he put his arms around her. He caressed her as if he were trying to discover the places she most inhabited – not romantically, but tenderly, with a sense of exploration. She was not aroused, exactly, but it was pleasant; it had been a long time since anyone had touched her like this.

She murmured, 'The way you touch reminds me of my mother.'

'How so?'

'Her touch is very seductive. I don't even like her, but when she starts to touch me, I suddenly become totally vulnerable to her. It's frightening.'

He liked this a lot. 'That's beautiful,' he said.

The intercom buzzed, announcing that they had ten more minutes. She 'took care of him' quickly, and they stood to dress. She stuck her feet back in her high heels, and cheerfully tore the sheets off the bed. He zipped up his pants, handed her an extra twenty and told her it had been a relaxing hour. She said yes, actually, it had been for her too, and then trotted off to stuff the wadded-up sheets in a reeking wicker basket. She walked him downstairs, feeling ungainly and knees-out in her tight skirt. She was aware of him looming and lurking darkly behind her as she came under the speculative, moody gaze of three potential Romeos.

'And here's Perry,' said Christine brightly.

'Hi,' she said, bobbing her head. She turned to Bernard and rolled her eyes as she walked him to the door, knowing that he would enjoy this open display of contempt.

'See you soon,' he said. He held her against him for a second, and she experienced a disorienting sense of comfort and safety that made walking back into the invading stares of her prospective boyfriends almost voluptuously exposing. She stood before them, and the canned laughter sounded once more.

That night she went to a group show at a small gallery in Soho that included work by her friend Sandra. As usual, she was one of the few non-artists there. Sandra, nervous and carefully chic in a bright blue pillbox hat and a long black velvet skirt, introduced her as 'my friend Stephanie, who writes for *The Village Voice*.' This impressed people, even when Stephanie said, 'I just wrote one thing for the *Voice* and that was a year and a half ago.'

'Yes, but you look like a writer for *The Village Voice*,' said a painter.

'That sounds like an insult to me.'

'It's not an insult, but it's not a compliment either.' He barked out a laugh.

Stephanie attached herself to another conversation about the embarrassing failure of an art gallery that she had never heard of, which, after a rapid shift of participants, became a discussion about somebody's review in the *Times* versus somebody's review in the *Voice*. Sandra rapidly crossed and recrossed the floor, darting in and out of conversations with apparent pleasure and animation. 'Nobody's *here*,' she hissed finally, near the hors d'oeuvres, even though there were dozens of people present.

Stephanie wandered from conversation to conversation, having an almost panicky feeling that although there were nice, interesting people in the room, the situation, for all its seeming friendliness and ease, precluded her from connecting with the nice and interesting aspects of them. She tried to figure out why this was and could not, beyond the sense that the conversations around her were opening and closing according to the subtle but definite rules that no one had told her about. Then she saw Dara, Sandra's other non-artist friend, standing regally alone. Dara was trying to become a fashion designer, and she looked unusually beautiful that night in a strapless satin dress that was dramatically faded in the middle where someone had probably spilled something on it a long time ago. Stephanie had always admired Dara, even though she was not friendly and had once been very rude to Stephanie on the phone. But Dara seemed pleased to see her and hung on to her presence throughout a shockingly dull conversation that stumbled awkwardly through Sandra's work, Sandra's husband's work, a writer Stephanie liked and a movie. Still, Stephanie resolutely held on to her idea of Dara as an interesting person. She said, 'You seem like someone who is at home in the world.'

A startled look flared in Dara's eyes; she glanced at Stephanie with disappointment. 'Nothing could be further from the truth,' she said shortly. 'I doubt you know anyone less at home than me.'

They stood silently, Stephanie's silence a disheartened one. She had thought she was making a penetrating remark that would impress Dara with her perceptiveness; instead she had revealed herself to be a person living in a dreamworld. This was always happening.

The next day at Christine's, she felt like a person in a dreamworld, specifically a *Playboy* cartoon dreamworld inhabited by beautiful, moronic prostitutes in short pink negligees lolling about on cushions with white cats while large men in suits smiled at them. It was a strangely pleasant sensation. It had been a slow afternoon, and the women lounged on the couch with their high heels off and their feet up, watching TV and eating heavily salted French fries from damp carry-out containers.

Stephanie was talking to Brett, an alert Chinese girl with waist-length hair. Brett had been in 'the business' for ten years, since she was seventeen, and she said she was ready to leave. She told story after story about how customers were always trying to take advantage of her, humiliate her or intrude on her sympathies in some grotesque way. 'It was just awful,' she said, concluding a particularly obnoxious story. 'It was as if he'd done it almost, having to listen to him say it, you know?' She leaned forward for a handful of French fries, stuck some in her mouth and chewed meditatively. 'When I was younger I had more energy to fight them off. No matter what they said or did, I could keep them away from my real self. But it gets harder and harder and I don't know how much longer I can go on. I want to do something else anyway. I'm bored.'

The other women began to talk about the terrible things men had done or tried to do, and how they'd thwarted them or gotten them back. There was a tenacious sense of defended pride in the room, which Stephanie felt both distant from and very much a part of. She thought of how pathetic this pride would seem to someone like Sandra, who had once disgustedly described a brief stint as a cocktail waitress as making her feel 'like a whore.'

The buzzer rang and Bernard the lawyer appeared, hands in his pockets, a sophisticated fellow playing the part, with mild amusement, of the casual businessman about to enjoy himself with a cheap woman. Stephanie smiled at him and sank back into the couch, feeling she was a sophisticated woman playing cheap. Soon they were back in the Shadow Room.

Trying to Be

'Do you remember those cartoons in *Playboy*?' she asked as they lay, not yet touching, on the bed. 'The ones about prostitutes with the same faces and bodies lying on pillows, wearing lacy nighties? And the men who were standing with flowers and chocolates in their hands?'

'Yes, of course.'

'It's funny, because I used to look at those things when I was ten and eleven years old and – well, I didn't really know what prostitutes were, but it looked like a good thing from what I could see in *Playboy*. They were beautiful and they didn't have to do anything but sit on cushions and men loved them. So I told my mother I wanted to be a prostitute when I grew up.'

'That's fabulous.' He smiled as though this was the most entertaining thing he'd heard all week.

'Naturally she freaked out, and my parents sent me to a psychiatrist.'

'Oh, good Lord.'

'But after a few visits the psychiatrist decided I was normal. I mean, I had good grades and friends and everything, so I didn't have to go anymore.' She shrugged. 'My poor sister wasn't so lucky. He had her on lithium by the time she was eleven.'

'But the psychiatrist was wrong about you, wasn't he?'

She laughed, but she thought: He was not wrong. I am actually pretty normal.

'So that's what you're doing. You're playing prostitute.' He stroked her face and hair.

She was startled that he seemed to be thinking in the same terms as she had been downstairs. She pictured him with his orange-haired, chain-smoking performance artist, and she had an almost visual sense of his delight in this educated woman who flew in the face of society, deliberately taking on a role that he probably considered demeaning, and then analyzing it. 'Actually, I'm not playing. This is for real. I'm not going to give you your money back.'

'You know what I mean.' He drew her against him and lightly scratched her head.

'But even as a kid I realized there were problems with the customer–hooker romance. Because once, when I was about twelve, I was in my father's study rubbing his neck – I used to do that all the time for him – and there was this *Playboy* calendar over his desk and some babe was on it and I said to him, "Do you like her?" and he said, "Sure I do," and I said, "Would you like to meet her?" and he looked shocked and said, "No, she's just a dumb broad." And I was appalled.'

Bernard's smile almost became a laugh. 'Well, but you know he was lying. He would've loved to meet her.'

'It's not funny. I was hurt by what he said. I was hurt for her.'

'No, I know it's not funny. I'm sorry.' He lay on top of her and kissed her, cupping her head tenderly in his hands. They kissed and touched each other and then broke apart to talk some more. She told him about the conversation with Brett and how it made her feel. She told him about the opening she had been to the night before, leaving out her almost frightened sense of isolation. She asked what his wife was like.

'She's intelligent, and very independent. She's better at being alone than I am. And she's adventurous in her own way. Last year she went to South America by herself, which isn't something most woman her age would do.'

'How old is she?'

'Thirty-nine.'

'What does she do?'

'Teaches high school, which she likes very much. I enjoy her, even if it isn't passionate. We actually have separate bedrooms.'

Trying to Be

'I couldn't be married like that,' she said. 'There would have to be passion.'

'You're very idealistic.'

'You're not?'

'No, I'm not. Anyway, marriage isn't about passion for me. We're excellent company for each other. And I don't want to be alone.'

They were silent for a moment; she gently felt his earlobes.

'Why do you come to places like this?' she asked.

'Why do you think?'

'I really don't know. How any grown man can accept what happens here as sex is beyond me. You could have affairs if you wanted, I'll bet. You don't seem that interested in sex here, anyway. So why do you come?'

'To meet fascinating creatures I'd never meet in the usual course of my life. Like you.' He touched her nose and smiled.

Of course, she realized what he liked about her. He loved the idea of kooky, arty girls who lived 'bohemian' lives and broke all the rules. It was the kind of thing he regarded with a certain admiration, but did not want to do himself. He had probably had affairs with eccentric, unpredictable women in college, and then married the most stable, socially desirable woman he could find. This did not make her feel contempt or draw away from him. She liked this vicarious view of herself; it excited and reassured her. She wasn't a directionless girl adrift in a monstrous city, wandering from one confusing social situation to the next, having stupid affairs. She was a bohemian, experimenting. The idea made rock music start playing in her head. She kissed him with something resembling passion.

'I would like to actually fuck you sometime,' he said. 'But

I don't think you enjoy sex here. I don't want it if you can't enjoy yourself.'

She smiled and tweaked the light layer of flab at his waist. 'But that doesn't apply to blow jobs, right?'

After he left, the day suddenly became very busy. Most of the men she saw were unpleasant, and she found herself taking refuge in the idea of Bernard the lawyer as she endured their malodorous company.

That night Sandra called her. Stephanie was sitting on her bed eating orange sorbet from a pint box and trying to view her life in a positive way, and she welcomed the interruption.

'Hi,' said Sandra. 'You're not writing, are you?'

'No, in fact, I was avoiding it.'

'Again?'

'I'm afraid so.'

Sandra sighed. 'Maybe you're trying to write at the wrong time of day. Most people have times of day when they're more productive than others. Have you considered that?'

'No, I haven't. Anyway, I have a job, you know.'

'That's right, I forgot. You don't have as much leeway as I do.' Sandra was supported by her husband, a painter whose father had given him a building. Stephanie had told Sandra that she was working as a maid for an agency that had several apartments on the Upper West Side. In her mind, this was grubbily close to the truth, and it rendered her conveniently unreachable by phone. She felt that Sandra viewed her fictional job with a mixture of secret repugnance and respect, astounded that a person she knew could do such a job without any apparent loss of self-esteem.

Sandra began to talk about the opening. After Stephanie had left, an important East Village art critic had arrived, and Sandra had hoped he would pay attention to her. But he

Trying to Be

ignored her completely and openly admired the work done by her friend Yolanda.

'I know it's petty, but by the end of the night, I could hardly speak to her. It's not just this one incident either; she's always getting attention – ever since she started putting those little beads in her hair and going out with that guy Serge. And I know what this sounds like, but sometimes I think people respond to her just because she's black and they want to prove they're not racist. I mean, I know she's good, but I work all the time, and she only does one painting every few months. And her stuff is derivative as hell. I mean, I know everybody's derivative in a way, but you know what I mean. It makes me feel like a piece of shit. Am I being awful?'

'Well . . . sort of,' said Stephanie, who thought Yolanda's work was clearly better than Sandra's. 'But I understand how you feel.' She told Sandra how annoyed she was when the name of a writer she didn't think much of began appearing in bold print in gossip columns everywhere. 'When I saw that picture of him in *Vanity Fair* at the Palladium with China Smith, I almost threw up,' she said.

They talked about how shallow and fake it all was, and once again Stephanie told the story of the twenty-three-year-old clerk who had driven her to despair with stories of his impending publication in *Esquire* and his subsequent book contract, until she found out that he was certifiably nuts and on lithium, and couldn't possibly be telling the truth.

Stephanie hung up feeling vaguely humiliated. She thought of her job at Christine's, almost so she could feel worse, but felt strangely comforted instead. This made no sense to her, but she accepted the comfort. She wished that she could tell Sandra about her real job, but she didn't dare. Perhaps Sandra wouldn't be shocked, but she would think it was self-destructive and insulting to women. Well, maybe it was. She never got any writing done while she was hooking. Somehow the idea of coming home after a day at Christine's and sitting down to write was impossible; her thoughts were clotted by the clamoring, demanding ghosts of the men she'd seen that day. She needed to make herself a nourishing meal and sit still and take care of herself, as her mother used to say. Working at Christine's was a time for making money and resting her brain, she told herself. Writing would come later.

She pictured herself in the future, so successful that she could talk about being a hooker without anyone minding. 'I didn't do much writing then,' she'd say to her circle of successful friends as they stood around smiling and holding their drinks. 'I spent most of my time just trying to re-form my personality.' And they'd all laugh at this adorable admission of her female vulnerability.

The only person she'd ever told was her friend from college, Babette. Babette, who was trying to be an actress, had a whole gaggle of friends from the restaurant where she worked who wore a lot of leather and went en masse to some S&M bar in the West Village on weekends. It didn't seem as though prostitution would faze Babette, but when Stephanie told her about her first experience three years earlier, she'd said, 'Oh, Stephie! How could you do that to yourself? How could you?' Stephanie explained again and again that she didn't think it was damaging her self-respect, but Babette would not be mollified. Stephanie suspected that Babette's consternation had little to do with self-respect and a lot to do with Babette's discomfort at discovering that she was friends with a prostitute instead of a writer. However, Babette was a fragile person who had done too much cocaine, had a breakdown, cut her wrist – shallowly, but still – and now saw a therapist twice a week, so she thought it was best not to speak to her again about subsequent episodes.

She didn't see Bernard during the next three days, but she saw a variety of people unappealing enough to demolish her soothing daydream of happy prostitutes and fatherly johns. One, although he had made a point of showering and vigorously drying beforehand, dripped sweat off the tip of his nose and onto her face as ardently as he dripped his endearments, and seemed genuinely puzzled, even hurt, when she turned away from his kiss. Another, a huge, morose fellow with a gold Pisces chain on his fleshy chest, lay on his back and talked about how the most wonderful time in his life had been when he played football in high school; he was unable to figure out why everything had been so boring ever since. 'I bet I know what you was like then,' he said, rolling over. 'You was one of them quiet types that never went out. And look at you now.' There was no malice in his voice; it was a wonderless comment, which made its accuracy all the more depressing. Then there was the concave-chested little person who so offended her with the pre-session suggestion that she 'suck his tits' that she involuntarily threw up her hands and said, 'No. No. Just no,' and walked out of the room and down the stairs, not caring whether or not Christine fired her, which she didn't. 'I'll send one of the other girls up,' she said to Stephanie as they huddled in the kitchen. 'You've worked hard today and I can afford to lose that geek if he walks.'

On the fourth day, when Bernard finally appeared, she fell into his arms. 'I'm so glad to see you,' she said, feeling his rather automatic placating response. She told him how terrible the last few days had been.

'This guy was there for half an hour droning about his

stupid high school days, and how important he was, and how all the cute girls would go out with him. It was just dreadful.' She noted Bernard's puzzled expression and laughed. 'I guess it doesn't sound so bad, but it really was. For a while I was in his life, and his life was lousy.'

He looked at her seriously. 'You're right,' he said. 'You shouldn't be here. This is a bad place for you.'

'I know. I'm going to quit next week.'

'If you do, you must give me your phone number. I'd really like to keep in touch with you. It doesn't have to be any big deal. I just think you're an interesting girl.'

She didn't see him before she quit, nor did he call her right away. When a week went by, she decided he'd changed his mind. She felt disappointed, but also relieved, and then stopped thinking about it. She eased back into her life slowly, first looking for another job and then trying to write every day.

Babette entered a period of energy and optimism and began asking her out to nightclubs again. Babette had a lot of friends in the club business, so they could unfailingly sail past the block-long lines of people vainly trying to catch some doorman's imperious eye. Babette, a tiny angular creature with long, slightly slanted eyes, looked annoyingly perfect in her silk Chinese jacket and black suede boots, her slim hip tilted one way, her little head the other. Stephanie always felt large and unraveled by comparison, as though her hat was wrong or her hem was falling out.

They could spend hours wandering through the dark rooms, holding their drinks and shouting comments at one another. Often they would meet friends of Babette's who would invite them into the bathroom for cocaine. Sometimes Babette would go off to dance and Stephanie would stand on the periphery of the dance floor, watching the dancers

Trying to Be

grinning and waving their arms in blind delight or staring severely at the floor as they thrashed their limbs. Lights flashed off and on, and the disc jockey spun one record after another in a pattern of controlled delirium. Stephanie would stroll through the club, watching the non-dancers blankly scrutinizing the dancers or standing in groups that were laughing with mysterious animation. After about fifteen minutes, she would be forced to face the fact that she was bored. Then she would remember what she was like before she came to New York and realize that this was what she had pictured: herself in a glamorous club full of laughing or morosely posing people. In frustration, she would decide that the reason it all seemed so dull was that she was seeing only the outermost layer of a complex society that spoke in ingenious and impenetrable signs to outsiders who, even if they were able to physically enter the club, were unable to enter the conversations that so amused everyone else. This was a discouraging idea, but it was better than thinking that the entire place was a nonsensical bore that people actually longed to belong in.

'Hi,' said a man with a hideous hunk of hair. 'I like your hat.'

'Thank you.'

'Would you like to dance?'

'No, thank you.' She looked right at him when she said this, meaning to convey that she didn't consider him repulsive, but that she was deep in thought and couldn't dance.

It didn't work; he stared away with a ruffled air and then said, 'Do you want to go to the Palladium?'

'No, thank you.'

He looked at her with theatrical scorn and she noticed that he was actually very handsome. 'Are you French?' he asked.

'No. Why do you ask? Do I sound French?'

'I don't know. You just look like you might be. Are you a dancer?'

'No. Why?'

'I don't know. You have to be something.' He looked as if he was about to spit.

'What do you do?' she asked.

'I'm an architect. Do you want some coke?'

'No, thank you.'

He looked at her as though she were completely mad and walked away. She quickly moved off the spot of this encounter toward a roomful of people in groups, determined to hear at least part of an interesting conversation. She was stopped by a man who wanted to know if she was Italian. She said no and escaped him. She was continuing toward a courtly group of large, aging transvestites who were the most welcoming and companionable bunch she'd seen all night when a very handsome black man took her elbow and said, 'Bonsoir. Are you French?'

'No.'

'Italian?'

'No.'

His faced changed a shade. 'What are you?'

'I'm from Illinois.'

He dropped her elbow with unmistakable contempt and turned his back to her. That was the last straw. She walked out of the club and into the street, not even bothering to look for Babette.

She walked ten blocks in her high heels, and was almost home when she decided to stop at a neighborhood lesbian bar. It would be comfortable, she thought, to get drunk in the company of jovial women. And it was, until a pleasant conversation she thought she was having turned into a nasty

Trying to Be

argument, before she ever saw the turn, about whether or not bisexual women are lying cowards. Then she staggered home.

At twelve o'clock the next day she answered the phone, making her voice as feeble and throaty as possible, the better to parry Babette with a muddled excuse. She didn't recognize his voice right away, not even when he mentioned Christine's, and he was beginning to sound insulted when she finally said, 'Oh, *hi*,' her voice wobbling pleasingly (to her) and making her feel like a tousle-haired, mascara-smeared movie babe in a rumpled bed. He was in the neighborhood, and he wanted to meet her for lunch.

'Gosh, I'd like to, but I was out late last night, I'm still in bed and I look awful.'

'Well, I'm disappointed, but maybe some other time.'

'Well, maybe I could . . . where are you?'

Half an hour later she was sitting with him in an expensive eggs Benedict place, with waiters in black pants mincing about as a piped-in symphony identified this as a haven of Western civilization. 'I tried to call you before, but you weren't at home and then I got incredibly busy. There's been a lot of fuss over a particular couple of blocks in the Village.'

'I've heard,' she said. 'Actually, I wish they weren't doing that to the Village. It's going to be awfully sterile soon.'

'That may be,' he said easily. 'But it would be sterile, not to say precious, if the old neighborhood were artificially maintained.'

'Letting a place alone isn't the same thing as artificial maintenance. Anyway, this is artificially accelerated development.' She argued with him happily, pointing out that he was contradicting an earlier-expressed belief that the government should manipulate the economy to protect the poor.

'Yes, I suppose you're right about that,' he said after her short speech. His indifferent capitulation left her forceful argument charging foolishly toward a vanishing target, and she changed the subject, telling him about the previous night. He especially liked the drunken argument with the lesbian, and said 'fabulous' three times.

Their eggs came in oblong dishes. The piped-in woodwinds sang stirringly of decency and order.

'What are you doing now that you've left Christine's?' he asked. 'Are you working or writing?'

'Neither one, really.' She thought: I'm trying to re-form my personality. 'I'm looking for a job, probably some clerical thing. Maybe something part time.'

'Have you considered something in an editorial capacity?'

'I tried that when I first came here and it didn't work out.'

'Why not?'

She shrugged. 'I guess I wasn't really interested enough.' She thought of trying to explain herself further, but ate her eggs instead. She remembered herself newly arrived in New York, nervously planning her future. She saw the ensuing events as a series of comic-strip pictures separated by dark borders. This was especially true of her job search – there she was, the round-shouldered applicant before the monotonous, large-handed boss. She remembered her interview with the most respected editor of the most prestigious publishing house in town:

'Oh, yes, I remember Georgia Helman.' The editor had rolled his eyes as he mentioned the woman who had referred Stephanie to him, a woman who had been his associate for two years. 'A rather pathetic case. The only reason I hired her was as a favor to a personal friend. She was so messed up with drugs and men, you know. But about you.' He looked at her as if she'd already been in his office several times. 'If you really want to be a writer, then don't move to New York. You'll just wind up in some dank little dump in the East Village with bars on the windows, and oh, I don't know.' He grimaced and flapped his hand with distaste.

She reminded him that she had already moved to the city and he said, 'Well, in that case, maybe you should try *The New Yorker*. They generally hire only friends and family, but you have a certain, I don't know, fresh, insipid look they might like. I've gotten quite a few people in there. Would you like to have a drink tomorrow evening?'

She had to admit that a large part of the reason she was even trying to get a job was for the approval of people she'd known in Illinois, many of whom were living in New York and thought of her as a hopeless neurotic who couldn't do much of anything.

She thought of her last conversation with one of these people, a film production assistant on her lunch break. 'Stephanie,' she said, 'you've simply got to cut your hair. I know it sounds superficial, but really, things like that matter. Editors are very busy people; they can only see you for twenty minutes, so they have to act on impressions, and that includes style. Long hair is college – ideals, finding yourself, and all that. Nobody here has long hair.' She dug smartly into her pile of refried beans.

She thought of Jackson, an ex-lover whom she had especially wanted to impress, and was perversely glad that she never did get a professional position. She remembered what a curious relief it had been to take her first job in a whorehouse, where a real job didn't matter, where males and females performed the ancient, primal and wonderfully elementary dance of copulation, blandly, predictably and by appointment.

'Is something wrong?' asked Bernard.

'I was just thinking of someone.' She hesitated. 'Someone I knew in college. I had a pretty awful relationship with this person and I couldn't have sex for over a year afterward. The first time I fucked anybody else after him was my first trick in my first house.'

'You're kidding!'

She laughed. 'It's too corny, isn't it? Girl has heart broken by callous swine and turns to prostitution.'

'Your life is very dramatic,' he said pleasantly.

'It's not so dramatic. These things happen. I mean, I'm over it now.'

Bernard walked her back to her building, but to her surprise he didn't want to come up to the apartment, even though she would have liked him to. In fact, they didn't fuck until the second time she had dinner with him. It was a calm, affectionate event ('I don't want to hurt you,' he said, referring to his problematic size as he lay on top of her, gripping her firmly about the hips). The evening was marred only when he handed her a hundred dollars on his way out the door.

She stared at him, stricken. 'I don't want that,' she said. 'That's not why I'm seeing you.'

He looked embarrassed. 'I know it's not why you're seeing me. It's not why I'm seeing you. But I think you should have it.'

'I don't want it.'

He sat on the bed. 'Stephanie, it's very simple. I have a lot of money. You do not. You need money. I can give it to you. Please take it.'

'You didn't give me money when we went out to dinner.'

He groped for an explanation for this and gave up. 'Well, the next time we go out to dinner, I'll give you money.'

'I won't take it.'

'If you don't, I'll just mail it to you.'

Accepting the money became less troublesome than arguing. She stared at the cash sitting on her dresser after he left and thought: So now it is my real life. Then she got up and put it in her wallet.

The next few times she saw him, the cash factor didn't seem so bad. It even felt perversely glamorous; it made her think of Babette's friend Natalia, a dark, striking girl who was trying to be an actress. Babette was always telling Stephanie, with a certain awe, how Natalia collected men who bought her clothes and gave her money and drugs. If only Bernard would buy her a dress or something, perhaps it would seem less dubious, but she enjoyed his company, he was sexually pleasant, and she rather relished the novelty of the situation, much as he probably did. She told her friends that she was seeing a married man who 'gave her money sometimes.'

'Stephanie, that sounds really good for you,' said Sandra. 'Sometimes it's good to have somebody who will just come over to your house and be nice to you.'

'I like that,' said Bernard as he held her in his arms. 'I'm a person who comes over to your house and is nice to you.'

Besides, it had been three weeks since she'd quit Christine's, and she still hadn't found a job, so the money was useful to her. Sometimes it was a hundred, sometimes two or even three hundred, depending on nothing but his mood.

Her days began to slide together in a passive slur of afternoon movies, galleries and nightclubs. Babette would ask her if she'd started writing and she'd say that she was taking notes, which was true. She was content to drift, confident that her unconscious was unconsciously gathering information.

She was having coffee in Soho one afternoon when Jackson walked into the café. He had the same mincing, narrow walk, the same rigid pelvis, the same uptilted chin. He looked at her and she at him. She held her breath. He quickly examined her, from foot to eye, and sat down on the other side of the room without answering her nod.

She thought of something Babette had said when Stephanie had told her about her first hooking experience. 'Oh, Stephie, don't you know this is exactly what Jackson said you'd do? How can you fall into that horrible idea he had of you?'

She had stiffly explained to Babette that this had nothing to do with Jackson, and she was sure that it didn't. But it made her feel bad to think of Jackson's reaction if he ever heard about it. The last time she'd seen him in New York, she had called him. He said they should meet for lunch, but lunch turned out to be a plastic glass of orange juice in a coffee shop while Jackson waited for his laundry to come out of a machine. He didn't have much time, he said. He was meeting his fiancée's parents at five. Their forty minutes of conversation were filled with pauses and downward looks. 'People in New York are very busy,' he said. 'I divide my time sparingly between my work and my social life. I find myself associating primarily with other young professionals.'

She told Bernard about seeing Jackson that night, as they sat in a loud bar having BLTs and drinks.

'It sounds romantic in a way,' he said. 'Silently passing each other in a crowded room.'

'It was awful.'

'What was so terrible about what happened between the two of you?'

She shrugged. 'It's hard to describe. I guess it's basically that corny thing I talked about. I loved him, I trusted him too much and he turned out to be a dreadful person.' She realized that Bernard was being distracted by a plump blonde with loopy earrings and white go-go boots. She paused until he turned toward her again. 'But it was more complicated. He had a lot of power over me. He was bisexual – don't worry, I test negative – and he was seeing this guy André at the same time that he was seeing me. Sometimes he'd literally get up out of my bed and go be with André. Then he decided André and I should be friends and that we should all go out together.'

'Why did you go along with this? Did you like it?'

'Yeah, that was part of it. I wanted to be open. I wanted to experience everything. And I loved Jackson, or thought I did. Eventually, I wound up in bed with both of them, and that's when it got ugly. I freaked out, Jackson decided I was boring and dropped me. That's it.'

Bernard stared at her more intently than he ever had, with a deepening, almost gloating shade of something she couldn't read in his dark eyes. He clasped her hand under the table and held it tight.

'Even after he left Evanston, I felt as if the whole tone of my time there was set by my thing with him. Everybody there knew about the three of us. Everywhere I went I got these looks. Jackson had a lot of friends who weren't the most compassionate people in the world and . . . it was painful.'

'But didn't such a complex liaison make you all the more mysterious and interesting to people?'

'I don't know. I didn't give a shit about being interesting and mysterious. I wanted him to love me.'

For a second, he looked as though she had said something truly strange. Then his face smoothed over with fatherly tenderness. He stroked her cheek. 'You really are a classic,' he said. 'You don't look it, but you are.'

Three weeks after she'd started seeing Bernard, a month after she'd left Christine's, an unexpected thing happened. Someone from a magazine she had interviewed with when she had come to New York three years before called her about a position as an editorial assistant. They had found her résumé and clips from the Evanston college paper in an old file and wanted to know if she was available. It was an architectural journal – not a subject she cared much about, but she remembered the magazine as being well written and beautifully designed. Besides, she was becoming desperate for a job, so she had the interview and was hired two days later.

Babette and Sandra seemed to think that it was the most wonderful thing in the world. (Now Sandra no longer had to stretch Stephanie's connection with the *Voice*, and could introduce her as 'in editorial.') Stephanie wasn't sure that it would in fact be a lot better than working at Christine's; she no longer cared about being a 'young professional' for Jackson's sake.

Meanwhile, her odd relationship with Bernard was beginning to trouble her. Their conversation, although they spoke of many things, seemed mostly polite and for the benefit of fantasies they had about each other. Sexually, they seemed to be on the same level. She couldn't tell if this was disappointing to him or not. And the money issue was beginning to disturb her again, now that she was working for the magazine. He's not someone who comes to my house and is nice to me, she thought as she lay alone in bed. He's someone who pays me to fuck him. She had an image of herself, sprawled half on and half off a bed at Christine's, her upside-down head patiently looking back at her from the mirror as some galoot humped her. This vision blended discordantly with the idea of herself at her desk at the magazine and she was unable to separate them.

Despite this ambiguity, she was curiously reluctant to drop the affair. He only saw her once or twice a week, he was not demanding, he liked her favorite authors and was somehow very reassuring. Reassuring of what, she didn't know, but it was connected to her old feeling that he thought of her as a representative of the exciting avant-garde – although it also seemed that if he had any brains at all, he would've realized by now that she was just a bewildered human.

'I think I know why you go to places like Christine's,' she said.

'I'm all ears.'

'One of the times I was there, I was watching this girl called Marissa, a skinny, not very attractive girl with blank brown eyes. It was almost the end of the night and she was squatting on the floor with her skirt hiked up to her waist, counting her money with a little furry-animal look of concentration, and I thought about how she must look to someone like you, despite her nasty personality – like this cute little beast who can be swept up and fondled and experienced and then put down.'

'That's fabulous.' He looked deeply entertained. 'You have such a wonderful way of expressing things.'

She thought: If he says 'fabulous' one more time tonight, I may punch him in the nose.

It was a cool autumn evening. Clawlike leaves smelling of ashes rasped and scuttled across the pavement as they walked to her apartment.

They were silent and she felt uncomfortable about it. They were returning from a dinner that should've been nice but wasn't. Bernard had been distracted and (she felt) bored by her. He had flirted subtly with their waitress, which she'd observed with a detached sense of disappointment, a cold and lifeless form of jealousy. As they mounted the stairs, she felt they were heading toward a destination simply because it was more trouble than it was worth to avoid it.

Once inside the warm apartment, though, she felt better about him, and she sensed a similar change in his mood. They lay snuggled on her bed and told short stories about their lives. He mentioned a girl he'd had a particular passion for in college, a headstrong dancer with long red hair, and told how he had finally seduced her one night after a party. 'It was one of the most exciting experiences of my life. At the last moment she panicked and said, "No, let me just take you in my mouth."'

'Why didn't she want to screw?'

'Because she felt too vulnerable and didn't want me to enter her.'

'What happened?'

'Well, I fucked her.' Pause. 'And that was the beginning of a long and intense relationship.'

'Did you ever consider marrying her?'

What a silly idea, said his face. 'No, no. I wasn't thinking about that then.'

'Did you ever feel a passion like that for your wife?'

'No, I really didn't. She was by far the most beautiful of all the women I'd been with, but I wasn't nearly as attracted to her as I had been to the others.' He touched her nose. 'You're really concerned about that, aren't you?'

They kissed and petted, and her absurd bed creaked. Then they separated and talked again. She told him about the time her sister's boyfriend had tried to seduce her in the middle of their breakup.

'What happened?' He smiled.

'Nothing. I didn't want to. I mean, I wasn't attracted to him and he was obviously doing it out of hostility to my sister.'

'Oh, no. That probably had nothing to do with it.'

'Well, maybe not. I think part of it was that he was intrigued by me as a variation of her.'

'Exactly!' He said this with great emphasis, as though she'd hit upon something important. 'I almost seduced my wife's sister the first time we separated, but we both balked at the last minute, mostly her. We were at the kitchen table, drinking gin.' He smiled. 'Of course your sister's boyfriend wanted you. One wants them all.'

She began to talk about an old lover of hers who reminded her of Bernard, but as she talked she kept imagining Bernard on a clean tiled kitchen floor, humping his blond wife's blond sister. It reminded her of the stories in *The New Yorker* about decent professional people having extramarital affairs. The more she contemplated this picture, the more difficult it was to imagine sex with this man . . . this customer. She had a quick feeling of sympathy for his wife, lying in her single bed, in her separate room, next to the room of a man who wanted them all. She started to feel something like guilt, and to forestall it, she began to kiss him. The bed creaked and he parted her legs.

From that moment on, the same sense of disaffection that she'd felt in the restaurant overtook her. Afterward, they spoke some more, but the conversation didn't work. They even had a strangely snide argument about whether or not Nabokov was a good writer. In the frequent silences, she felt that he sensed her sudden disapproval of him. She was a little sorry, because she liked him, but at the same time she was relieved when he got up to go. When he said 'Take good care of yourself,' she knew that she wouldn't hear from him again.

It wasn't until half an hour after he'd left that she realized that for the first time he hadn't left her any money. This had an entirely unexpected effect on her; she sat on her bed and cried.

She couldn't have said what she was crying about. Christine's, Brett, Jackson, her first miserable, lonely year in New York and Bernard the lawyer all seemed to have something to do with it, although she couldn't tell if she was just pulling anything available into her sadness. She cried until she was sure she was absolutely finished. Then she got up, put on her shoes and went out for a walk.

It was a beautiful Halloweenlike night, and there were exuberant people on the streets. She walked happily, admiring faces and haircuts. She looked at people, dogs, cars and buildings, and everything pleased her. She stopped at a Korean grocery store and looked at the fruit. She was struck by how neat and beautiful it was in its organized, traditional piles. She thought of herself coming here every week and buying fruit, vegetables, bread, cereal and milk, and it seemed like a wonderful idea. She bought herself an apple, and walked home eating it.

The Dentist

In Jill's neighborhood there was a giant billboard advertisement for a perfume called Obsession. It was mounted over the chain grocery store at which she shopped, and so she glanced at it several times a week. It was a close-up black-and-white photograph of an exquisite girl with the fingers of one hand pressed against her open lips. Her eyes were fixated, wounded, deprived. At the same time, her eyes were flat. Her body was slender, almost starved, giving her delicate beauty the strange, arrested sensuality of unsatisfied want. But her fleshy lips and enormous eyes were sumptuously, even grossly abundant. The photograph loomed over the toiling shoppers like a totem of sexualized pathology, a vision of feeling and unfeeling chafing together. It was a picture made for people who can't bear to feel and yet still need to feel. It was a picture by people sophisticated enough to fetishize their disability publicly. It was a very good advertisement for a product called Obsession.

At least this is what Jill thought about it, but Jill was an essayist who wrote primarily for magazines, and she was prone to extravagant mental tangents that were based on very little. She had to be, in order to keep thinking of things to write about. Besides, she was perhaps hypersensitive to the idea of obsession, as she had just become obsessed with someone. He was a mild, pale, middle-aged man who did not return her ardor, and what should've been a pinprick disappointment had swollen into a great live wound that throbbed at night and deprived her of sleep, of thought, even of normal physical sensation.

'Drop it,' said her friend Pamela. 'Don't even, as they say, think about it. He sounds really fucked up, and not in an interesting way. There wouldn't be any satisfaction for you. It would be like jerking off forever and not coming.'

It was. She would lie curled on her bed, making sounds of animal pain, dry even of tears, as thoughts of the loved one so feverishly inflated her desire that she could not fit it into a fantasy which she could then make end in at least rote physical satisfaction.

The odd thing was that the object of her inflated feelings was her dentist.

The terrible situation had begun when she had gone to have a wisdom tooth removed. Jill was thirty-seven, and her one remaining wisdom tooth had had ample opportunity to grow where it didn't belong, for example, around her jawbone. Neither she nor the dentist had realized this at the onset of the operation, and he had, in a professionally somnolent voice, assured her that the ordeal would probably be over in fifteen minutes. An hour later, the as yet mercifully unsexualized dentist was still gripping her jaw with enough force (as it turned out) to bruise her, perspiring and even grunting slightly as he tore her tooth out bit by tiny bit.

'It became almost comic,' she said later. 'He kept heaving back, sort of panting with exertion, and he'd say, in that voice of inhuman dentist calm, "Just a little more; we're going to move it around in there just a little bit more, and then I think we've got it." It got to the point where I could smell him sweating, and a certain indecorous tone crept up under that professional voice, a sort of hysteria straining at the borders. Finally, when he started to give me the speech one last time,

I snapped, "I just want the fucking thing out." And he snarled back, "Okay," totally ripping the lid off the calm facade, which is probably pretty hard-core for a dentist.'

'And that's when you got excited?' asked Pamela.

'No. No, I felt united with him in disbelief and disgust at the whole thing, but I was certainly not excited. That didn't happen until later.'

A few days after the tooth came out, there were complications. She developed an infection and had to return to the dentist's office twice. She had an allergic reaction to the pain medication he prescribed for her, and to make up for the unpleasantness, he gave her free medication out of his closet. The gift pills didn't make her itch, but they made her pulse lunge and her mind twist, so that she was too disoriented to write a commissioned piece for a fashion magazine on the torment of having small lips. With a great effort, she decided not to become discouraged and instead sat down to type a long handwritten draft of a two-part series on whether or not people's memories of being abused as children are real. She had typed the first line when her word processor collapsed.

Her word processor was so old and primitive that no local repair company would service it, and it would take weeks for the whimsical midwestern manufacturer to do it, what with shipping and all. No computer she could rent, borrow, or buy could read the old monster's disks. Besides, she couldn't afford to buy another machine, and since she had recently moved to San Francisco from Boston, she did not know any writers from whom she could borrow one, and she was not confident about her ability to use a new one anyway. Right about then her jaw started to throb through the pain medication. 'I'm tearing my hair out,' she said to Pamela, and it was close to the truth. She couldn't pay that month's rent, she was lonely, she had bad dreams, she was worried about losing her looks, and her jaw hurt like hell.

There is nothing like physical pain for enlarging and enhancing free-floating emotional pain. As she walked to the dentist's office, Jill began to feel desperate. She was maddened by the noise and motion of the street, she was irritated by the sweet spring air. A burst of purple flowers on a dirty white wall shocked her with their brightness and lulled her with their low whisper of the deep earth, making her feel pulled in two directions and unable to go in either.

'Well, you've got a dry socket,' said the dentist, drawing back from her with a mournful, empathic air. 'It's something that *can* happen sometimes, and it's nothing to worry about, although it *can* be quite painful. We'll just increase the pain medication and pack the area nice and tight. Then it's up to you to keep off that sensitive area.' He paused. 'I'm sorry you've had to walk around with it hurting so much. With that exposed bone, I frankly don't know how you stood it.'

'I *can't* stand it,' she said. She hesitated, fearing that she was perhaps tastelessly spewing into the dentist's vast spaces of professional calm. Then she decided that with all that vastness, he could afford it, and she spewed hard. 'It's not just the tooth. It's everything. I can't sleep. I can't talk to anybody. I'm going broke and I can't write my articles because I'm in a drug haze. I can't even type an article, because my stupid word processor broke and I can't afford another one. And now you're telling me it's going to keep being like this for days more. I don't know what to do. I don't know what to do.'

'I can loan you my laptop,' he said. 'No problem.'

She paused to adjust to the sudden shift in terrain. 'I don't know how to use a computer.'

'It's easy,' he said. 'I'll teach you.'

The Dentist

She looked into his gray eyes. They were opaque with dutiful kindliness. He wants to be my friend, she thought. Probably he's not thinking sex; he's not the type. I'll just have to be friendly with him, which is a pain, but if I can type that article, the activity will make me less hysterical.

'I could bring it by tomorrow evening,' he offered. 'It's no trouble at all.' His voice was like a stream of lukewarm water running over her wrist.

'All right,' she said slowly.

'And he did it,' she said to Pamela. This was much later, after the grueling drama had erupted. 'He did exactly what he said. I felt sort of guarded when he first came in, but I saw right away it wasn't necessary. He set the thing up, showed me how to work it, and *left*. He was like a UPS man or an electrician. I think even the cat was impressed with his discretion.'

'Was he friendly?'

'More like beneficent. Actually it was this combination of beneficence and self-conscious goofiness. He carried the computer to my desk with this proud little outthrust of his chest in front and this silly little outthrust of his butt in back. Like he was performing a skit he'd done a thousand times before and was still just bemused enough to do again.'

Pamela uttered a cautious, noncommittal sound. She lived in New York and, as Jill's oldest friend, had stood by her through many grueling dramas. But Jill hadn't gotten involved in anything *too* ridiculous for a few years, and Pamela seemed to find this recidivism depressing.

'When he left he said I could call him at any time of the day or night. If he was at work, his beeper would go off and he'd call me back.'

'Well, his behavior is strange,' said Pamela. 'Because he certainly gave you every reason to believe he was interested.'

The dentist's rigorous and polite reliability impressed Jill, who had not often seen such behavior in men. She had left home at sixteen to live with a commercial artist almost fifteen years older than she was, and although the affair only lasted three years, she left it in a state of unfortunate attunement to the kind of refined, convoluted fellow who likes to make a very fancy mess. She had put herself through school with five years of work in various strip bars and go-go joints, and, at the age of twenty-six, had entered into journalism with the publication of an essay about down-and-out jazz musicians in a trendy men's magazine. Because of the unusual career segue, she had few professional acquaintances and almost no experience with the sort of mundane camaraderie that makes up the common social staple; thus her baseline emotional life had consisted mainly of going from one loud mess to the next. To her, the dentist's simple and undemanding generosity looked like a shining piece of integrity, which aroused first her surprise and then her admiration. Admiration didn't develop into love right away, though, and the first time she called him, she did so reluctantly. It was, after all, one in the morning, but the computer had disobeyed her at a decisive moment, and he *had* said anytime.

He greeted her as if he had been waiting alertly for her call. As he solved her problem, their conversation dipped and bumped along easily. He complained mildly about difficulty he was having with a lab he used. He told her about an old movie he had seen on TV that evening, called *Hot Rods to Hell*, in which a father (played by Dana Andrews) is terrorized and humiliated by sexy youths but eventually triumphs over the youths. The dentist compared it favorably to newer humiliation / triumph-based movies he'd seen recently. His disembodied voice was gentle and authoritative, and had an undertone that sounded thwarted, feisty, and playful at once. She pictured him in an apartment made up of utilitarian oblongs, gray shadows, gleaming limbs of furniture, and an entertainment center, all alone with his thwarted feistiness.

'George?' she asked. 'Are you happy?'

'Pretty much,' he answered. 'Why wouldn't I be?'

She hung up feeling enveloped and upheld by his 'Why wouldn't I be?' His tone seemed to acknowledge all that might threaten happiness – 'It's something that *can* happen sometimes and it's nothing to worry about' – and then to shoulder it aside as if the important thing was to get through life somehow, to extract teeth, to follow the schedule, to do what you said you would do. This was a new point of view for Jill, and it affected her profoundly. She finished her article quickly and went to bed feeling an unfamiliar species of warmth and comfort. She woke imagining the dentist holding her from behind, and she prolonged the image, allowing it to become a thought.

That day she sent her article to the magazine that had commissioned it and, since her jaw was feeling better, arranged to have dinner with her friend Joshua. Joshua was a frustrated musician. He was frustrated mostly by himself. He had achieved a modest success in Boston and then come to San Francisco to pursue a hopeless infatuation with a lesbian who didn't even like him as a person. He claimed the experience had damaged his 'voice,' and now he worked as a cabdriver, occasionally managing a sit-in gig for some obscure band. Joshua was very intelligent and very dear, and like many people who have difficulty managing their own lives, his opinions and advice were often excellent. They went to a cheap Thai place in the Mission. Jill told the story of the dentist as if it were a funny joke.

'He's a total nerd,' she finished. 'He's the kind of guy who says "All righty" at the end of conversations. Of course, I'm not really attracted to him. But it's funny that the thought even crossed my mind, don't you think?'

'I don't know,' said Joshua thoughtfully. 'I can see it, actually.'

'See what? What's there to see?'

'Well, it's like – remember when those weird thieves broke into my apartment?'

He was referring to the time a spectacularly eccentric thief or thieves had broken into the house he shared with three other people and apparently meandered through it, stealing a scarf, two pairs of pants, an address book, a Sonic Youth tape, and the contents of the mailbox.

'They took my unemployment check, and I had to go through this ordeal of getting it canceled, which meant I had to officially sign up for benefits again. Which meant standing in line at the unemployment office and explaining my situation and being told I was in the wrong line – it went on all day, and still it wasn't fixed. And that's the kind of thing that drives me crazy.'

Jill murmured sympathetically.

'So I had to come back the next day and wait in yet another line. I was almost at the end of my rope when this woman who worked there overheard me talking to another clerk about it, and she said, "Come over here, I'll help you." And not only did she help me, but she turned the whole experience into this really nice exchange.'

'Was she good-looking?' asked Jill.

'Not especially. She was a middle-aged woman with a smart haircut. She had on a nice blouse with tiny polka dots, which I always like. But what really made me respond to her was that when these people just behind me in her line started bitching, she yelled out this funny comment off one of their complaints

The Dentist

and made them laugh. That opened up the experience and made it okay to be standing there in line. I felt really attracted to her because she could do that.'

'Enough to ask her out?'

He shrugged. 'It was more ephemeral than that. Sort of like what you're describing. But it was a great little moment.'

'Yeah,' she said. 'It is like me and the dentist. You and I are so inept at practical details that when the practical details are, like, exploding in your face, and suddenly there's someone who can not only straighten it out for you but who seems to embody a whole universe where these disasters are just taken in stride, you're going to be incredibly grateful. Like, yes, there is an emotional hell that can't be fixed, but on the other hand, there's the dentist and the unemployment lady working away making things go smoothly at least on some level.'

'And who also acknowledge the emotional hell,' said Joshua. 'Like the polka-dot lady with her joke.'

'Yes! Exactly.'

'What's interesting about the dentist, though . . .' Joshua paused, and his face became uncharacteristically sly. 'He's solved your problems, but he also caused them to a certain extent. I mean, he hurt you.'

They finished dinner and relocated to a dark little bar. They sat in a booth with sticky wooden seats and steadily drank. Joshua described a TV show he'd seen, about an experimental program being conducted by some prison systems that enabled victims and their families to confront the criminals who had victimized them. He described the emotional scene between a thief and the clerk he'd shot, each of them telling the other what the robbery had been like for him – the clerk refraining, 'Why did you do that to me?' until the robber apologized and they embraced with a great deal of emotion.

Jill was interested, but as she settled more comfortably into drunkenness, she found it hard to concentrate on the story; she was distracted by the memory of the dentist's disembodied voice issuing instructions over the phone. 'I want you to press "alt,"' he said inside her head. 'Good. Now I want you to go to file.'

'But the last confrontation was pretty nasty,' continued Joshua. 'It was between a woman whose daughter had been raped and murdered and the guy who did it. The mother was religious, apparently, and she kept trying to appeal to the guy on those terms. He seemed to have respect for religion, and a couple of times he said he was sorry for raping and killing the daughter. But he said it with this odd kind of reserve, this detached compassion for the poor old mom, and that just seemed to drive her crazy. She kept saying she wanted to know exactly what it had felt like to rape and strangle her daughter, and after a while he started to look at her like, "Hey, lady, who's the freak here?" And I have to say he had a point. But he couldn't remember anything about the murder or the rape, because he'd blacked out – which he also apologized for. The mom got more and more frustrated, and in this kind of masochistic frenzy she blurted out, "I know I should get down on my hands and knees and thank you for not torturing my baby." And a look of utter shock flashed in the killer's eyes, like two live wires had just been touched together inside him. He just stared at her. Like he *recognized* her. It was way creepy.' Joshua paused. 'The girl's father was there too. But he didn't say anything. He just sat there with his head down.'

The next evening she called the dentist. She pretended to have a question about the computer, and he said, 'I want you to press "alt." The banality, the politeness, and the harmless hint of command were all accentuated by the abstracted

The Dentist

context and took interesting forms in her imagination. Happily, she visualized all kinds of things he might want her to do.

When he finished instructing her, she asked him questions about himself. He told her that before dental school he had studied theater and film. He had done his undergraduate thesis on lesbianism among strippers – which, he confidently assured her, was quite high, at least in Scranton, Pennsylvania.

'Really,' said Jill. She felt slightly nonplussed without quite knowing why. 'What kind of show did they do?'

'Show?'

'You know, when they stripped.'

He told her that he had only interviewed the strippers and had not watched them perform.

'Why not?' she asked. 'I mean, weren't you curious?'

No, he wasn't.

'That should've been your first hint,' said Pamela. 'A twenty-some-year-old guy who's not interested in watching strippers but who wants to establish their lesbianism? He's either a pervert or he's pathologically frightened or he hates women. Or all three.'

'I don't know,' said Jill. 'I thought it might be something else with him. I was pretty surprised when he said it, but I thought maybe he was trying to be a feminist or something.'

When she finished her project, he brought her his printer.

'I must take you to dinner,' she said. 'You've been so incredibly kind.'

He demurred, making the expected mutterings about the least he could do. 'Besides,' he said, 'I like to help creative people.'

They went to an Italian place in North Beach. They stared at their menus with ritual concentration. In the public setting, the dentist looked like a stranger, and that unnerved her; vainly she tried to revive the mysterious frisson that had arisen over the phone. He was wearing a loose-fitting turquoise sweater and faded corduroy pants, the casualness of which gave him a rumpled, little-boy sensuality that was pleasing but overly sweet for her tastes.

'How old were you when you did your thesis on lesbian strippers?' she asked.

'Twenty-two. Why?'

'It's very unusual for a man that age to be so uninterested in watching women take off their clothes and gyrate. Especially if you were interested in whether or not they were dykes.'

'Have you ever been in one of those places, Jill? They're pathetic and –'

'I used to work in one, actually.' She paused so that he could say 'Really?' but he just sat there and blinked. Maybe, she thought, he had read it in a magazine bio note. 'I didn't think of it as pathetic, personally. Some of the women were worth seeing, I thought.'

'It wasn't the women who were pathetic; it was the men.' A certain professorial tone had crept into his voice. 'Sitting there slavering over women who were really lesbians anyway.'

'I'd just think . . . out of curiosity, if nothing else –'

'Look, during my second year of college I worked as an assistant cameraman for a low-grade porn company, and I wasn't interested in seeing any more naked women.'

'Oh,' she said. 'Well. That's –'

'And I was disgusted by the way the women were treated. Really bad.'

She pictured the young dentist standing in a nondescript basement holding camera equipment while all about him nondescript naked women assumed lewd poses. He was wearing the same beneficent, self-consciously goofy expression he'd worn when he'd first arrived at her home with his computer.

'But a strip show isn't necessarily the same as porn,' she said. 'At least not when I did it. It's more about watching someone's fantasy of themselves.' She paused. 'Unless of course you're gay.'

'No, I'm not.'

'Well, then –'

'Jill, I'm shy.'

'The funny thing was, when he said the thing about not wanting to watch strippers? It made me feel slighted, almost demeaned.' Jill was stationed on her bed in extended phone call position, bolstered by pillows, wrapped in a quilt, legs tensely curled into her chest. 'When he said he wasn't interested in seeing any more naked women, it was almost like he'd slapped me,' she said.

Joshua was silent for a moment. 'That's a very unusual reaction,' he said.

'I know it doesn't make sense,' she said. 'But I felt the same way when he talked about how terrible the porn people were. What he said seemed nice and even moral, but there was something . . . hostile in it.'

'Are you sure?'

'No, of course not. But I can't shake the feeling. It's infuriating. He's trying to put himself in this superior position. Like, here's these strippers, doing their all, and he's sitting there going tut-tut. Unlike the gross, pathetic men who *are* interested, he's scrutinizing it with a purely scientific eye, in order to ascertain exactly how many lesbians there are per strip joint. And if he's so disgusted by porn, what was he doing there? He was feeling superior, the smug fuck.'

'So I guess you don't like him anymore.'

'He told me he didn't like strip shows because he's shy,' she went on excitedly. 'But I don't buy that. Strip shows exist for shy men.'

'I don't know about that,' said Joshua. 'I'd be shy about going to a strip show. I mean, I could picture some huge, leering stripper putting her underpants over my face while brutish guys laugh.'

'Oh, come on, Joshua. You know it wouldn't be that good.'

But later that night, his plaintive joke had its effect. She lay in bed, fantasizing about the dentist lording it over a grinding stripper, then interposing it with another fantasy, in which he trembled in fear before her. Each image was affecting in its own way; together, they were dramatic and moving. The dentist was complicated and unusual, she thought, yet decent. Like her, he had done things not everyone could understand, and he was perhaps not sure what he felt about it all. She went into sleep imagining that she was leading the dentist up a gentle, grassy hill over which a primary-colored rainbow stoutly arched.

She woke the next day feeling very emotional. She decided she was going after the dentist whether he was a ridiculous love object or not. She went for a long walk, during which she brooded, toiling uphill and down, on how to best declare herself.

'I got him some flowers,' she reported to Lila, her hairdresser. 'And I brought them to his office.'

'That's so sweet,' said Lila as she moved efficiently about Jill's perched, enrobed frame. 'How did he respond?'

'Well, I was planning to just drop them off with his secretary, but he happened to be standing there by her desk when I walked in with them. He just gave me this glassy-eyed stare. His face looked frozen, like he was suppressing insane rage.

The Dentist

And then he looked normal and flustered.' Just beyond the dentist's shoulder, Jill had glimpsed the profile of a woman's head lying on the headrest of the reclining dental chair; her open mouth made her look stunned and victimized. 'He said thanks, I shouldn't have, and that he had to get back to work. He took them and just wandered off to some back room, while his secretary beamed. I figured, okay, he's not into it. But then he called that night and asked me to the movies.'

In fact, he had asked if she wanted to go to a body-piercing exhibition. She was surprised, as she would not have thought piercing was the dentist's kind of thing – it certainly wasn't hers, at least not as it would occur in the gaudy vacuum of a public exhibit. She said she'd rather see a movie, and they decided on an art film about a drug-addicted police officer who sexually abuses young girls.

The dentist arrived at her apartment an hour early, which was awkward as Jill had just emerged from the shower and had to answer the door in her bathrobe. Still, she chattered enthusiastically all the way to the theater, in spite of her crude, unkind thoughts when the dentist proudly described his car as 'the smallest in the world.'

She had hoped the vaunted sex scenes in the movie would provide a delicious cocoon of titillation and embarrassment that they could inhabit together. But she just felt embarrassed.

'I hated it,' she declared as they left the theater. 'I thought it was pretentious and boring, except for that one jerk-off scene. I have to admit, that wasn't bad.'

'I thought that went on a little long – for what it was,' said the dentist judiciously. 'And it was very unrealistic that the nuns they raped were all so good-looking.'

They went to a restaurant and talked about random minor subjects. Neither one of them, it seemed, was at ease.

The dentist's facial skin appeared strangely immobile, and although he looked at her, his eyes seemed shut from the inside. As if in reaction to his stillness, Jill's voice leapt and darted with an animation that embarrassed her and could not be restrained. She ordered glass after glass of wine. Her animation felt increasingly like a sharp object with which she vainly poked the dentist. What a boring person, she thought. I definitely don't want to have sex with him. This thought calmed her, and as they sailed back to her apartment in the smallest car in the world, she felt so calm that she wanted to put her head in his lap.

'Would you like to come in for a little bit?' she asked as he pulled up to the curb.

'I can't,' he said. 'I have to feed the dog.'

She took a deep breath and exhaled. 'Could you please come in for just a minute? It'll make me feel safer.'

'And that's exactly what he did,' she told Lila. 'He came in for a minute. He stood there while I fed the cat, and then he said, "Had fun. I'll call you," and left.'

'This guy really likes you,' said Lila.

'You think so?'

'Yeah.' Lila gazed at Jill's hair in the mirror, meditatively cupping its new shape with both hands. 'I think he likes you a lot.'

For the next week her octopus imagination wound itself about the dentist, experimentally turning him this way and that. But he remained obdurate and glassy-eyed in its sinuous grip, and eventually she released him with an exasperation that became forgetfulness.

She didn't even notice when he failed to call her; partly because of an emotional fight with an editor named Alex, which made her rage about the apartment, angrily talking to herself for days. Alex, with whom she had cultivated a rather tender friendship, had wanted her to write something about her sexual experiences, even though she hadn't had any for over a year. She was offended because she thought he was being exploitative, which offended him because he thought she was being judgmental and hypocritical as well – hadn't she, after all, written about being a stripper two years earlier? 'That was different,' she huffily explained to Joshua. 'That wasn't about stripping; that was about power struggles in relationships. Stripping was just the motif.'

Then her word processor returned, looking small and likable in its Styrofoam nest, and she was offered an unusual job writing text for a book of photographs by an artistic photographer, which would require her to travel to Los Angeles. The photographs would all be of a famous model known for her risqué public persona, and the model wanted some of them to be taken in a strip bar with a real stripper.

'We want a thousand words on illusion and transformation,' said the editor. 'We want your real-life take on it.'

Jill arrived at the strip joint at eight in the morning. Various assistants, looking tired and hungover, worked at arranging elaborate camera equipment or stood with an air of taxed authority over portable tables of makeup. The model was sequestered in her trailer, and the famous photographer was shooting the stripper as she walked on a table. The photographer told the stripper she was beautiful. She wasn't, and appeared to know it, but the photographer said she was again and again until she finally, shyly, began to carry herself as if she were. The owner of the place sat behind the bar, nursing an early cocktail and desultorily jeering his employee. 'Take it off!' he weakly cried.

'She doesn't have to take anything off.' The photographer spoke in the proud tone of a mother. 'She's perfect just as she is.'

'The big star,' muttered the owner.

'Shut up, Nelson,' said the stripper. 'If she says I'm beautiful, then I'm beautiful.'

'Silly bitch,' he replied.

The photographer turned sharply. 'Don't call her a bitch,' she snapped.

'It's okay,' said the stripper mildly. 'I am a bitch.'

The model entered in the full splendor of her great height and conferred glamour. 'Wow, there she is!' bawled the stripper. 'Yeah!'

As the model and the stripper posed together, Jill drank coffee with a set of superfluous assistants, listening while the model asked the stripper about her life. For example, did her boyfriend object to what she did for a living?

'Boy, that light sure is hell on the old cellulite,' said Jill.

'We were just saying the same thing,' responded an assistant.

During a break, Jill questioned the model about why she wanted to pose in a strip joint.

'These women are so interesting to me,' she said. 'Their lives are totally degrading – but are they really so different from us? I'm saying, Look, let's have some compassion.'

Jill remarked that she had not felt degraded when she was a stripper, which seemed to surprise the model.

'Well,' she said, 'there's a lot of denial. There has to be, in order to survive.'

The crew was still engaged in a disorderly departure when the bar opened for business. The lone customer did not seem to notice the harried people carrying camera equipment. He just sat there with a drink in his hand and stared at the stripper, who had taken off her G-string and was bending over to look between her legs at him. He looked completely uninterested, but still he sat there and stared. When the song was over, he handed the girl two dollars. She came off the stage, holding the two dollars and griping about the lousy tip. There was humiliation in her griping, but there was also feistiness, and the combination was lovable. Jill tried to figure out why it was lovable and couldn't, except that it was an interesting combination of collapse and ascendancy. Jill thought the dentist might really like the stripper. She was, after all, a lot like him, yet he could feel superior to her.

On the plane back to San Francisco, she imagined talking with the dentist about the experience. She didn't imagine anything more than a conversation, but she so layered this conversation with the pleasure of understanding and being understood that it became a fantasy of mental sensuality: she and the dentist would rub their brains together. Together, they would pick apart each strand of the model's show of compassion and daring juxtaposed with the stripper's humiliation and guts juxtaposed with the customer's bland compulsive staring and the editor's relentless practicality. It was a cornucopia of contrasts and bursts of personality and slithering emotional undercurrent, from which they could select the strands that made their inmost strands vibrate and hum. And they would feel the vibrating and humming in their voices, deep under their ordinary words. For days she cherished this fantasy, even as it faded like a favorite rough spot on the inside of her mouth.

Then he called her. Her impulse to vibrate and hum was pretty well exhausted by then, but still his voice aroused it, even though his voice was jocular and empty. It was fun to talk about the stripper and the model. He loved the stripper's saying, 'I am a bitch,' and he liked the part where she bent over in the guy's face. He didn't say he liked it, but his voice became warm and friendly, as though he were being rubbed. Jill got stuck for a moment on the complexity of it; was he responding that way because he was enjoying the idea of someone in a degrading situation or was he too feeling the lovable feistiness bleeding through the story? Both of them enjoyed condemning the model and the vulgarity of the project. Jill complained about being forced to write something charming about such a false and manipulated experience, and she infused her complaints with a flirtatious petulance that invited him to compare her to the undertipped stripper. She wallowed in a sense of voluptuous connection through mutually acknowledged degradation, and she thought he did too. He said he was very busy but that he'd call her sometime and they could go to a movie.

That night she thought of the dentist again. She wanted her thoughts to be tender and kind, like they had been the first time she'd thought of him. But they weren't. Try as she might, she could not imagine him touching her, or even being close to her. She couldn't imagine him going away, either. Whichever way she turned, his face and his eyes stayed before her, staring with a masklike fixity that was both intense and detached. There was a hint of contempt and a hint of fascination in his face, except that, in her mind's eye, those feelings were too stilted to properly be called feelings. The image made her both desperate and numb, and, under that, other feelings oscillated too rapidly for her to identify them.

By the morning, she was sick of the dentist. Grimly, she directed her thoughts at the essay she was supposed to write; when they moved elsewhere, she supervised them sternly. But whatever they touched upon, she felt the dentist lurking beneath. She remembered Joshua's story about the mother confronting her daughter's rapist and killer. She imagined the incoherent weeping mother and the killer sealed away in his politeness. She imagined the killer's eyes sparking with recognition as the mother stepped out of her territory and onto his. She imagined telling the dentist about it, over and over again.

Every night during the next week the dentist stared at her from inside her head. Eventually, she got used to it and slept through it, the way one can learn to sleep through a persistent noise. Any day, she thought, he would call and they would talk and their words would gradually diffuse the potency of the image. But he didn't call, and his absence polarized his imaginary presence, making it both more vague and more powerful, so that it seeped through all her thoughts and feelings whether or not she visualized him at night.

She tried to remember what she had liked about him. She had thought he was kind and discreet. His kindness still seemed real, but it was mixed with elements she wasn't sure of. His discretion now seemed like a remoteness so intense it was almost fierce. To receive kindness combined with such remove was like receiving an anonymous caress while blindfolded.

She went on a magazine assignment to see a performance piece by a masochist who tortured himself onstage in various complex and aesthetically pleasing devices of his own making, while he made jokes and talked about his childhood. His childhood was significant in that he had cystic fibrosis and thus experienced pain, frustration, and social humiliation very early on, which, he felt, had prepared him for a life of masochism – and for which he was therefore grateful. 'It's not about anger or self-hate for me,' he said. 'It's like a kind of spiritual jujitsu. It's like, you give me pain? I'll take it to the hundredth power.' He was a vulnerable and compelling person, desiccated, scarred, and rather luminous in spite of being quite puffy from cortisone shots. Several people in the audience were so moved by him that they wept. When he drove a nail through his penis, one man passed out.

That night, she dreamed about a tattooed man whose face and body had been ornamentally pierced many times over. They walked up a hill, on a beautiful wooded path. The man was naked to the waist, and he had the masochist's slim, starved, scarred torso. His face was hollow, and the hollowness invited her in. Their entire conversation consisted of him pretending to want to touch her and then backing away. She eventually became angry. 'Oh,' he said. 'But you are very special to me.' And, as if to illustrate that sentiment, he opened his mouth and a bird flew out. It hung in the air, frozen like an iconic carving.

She decided to see a therapist, even though she would have to put it on a credit card. The therapist was a small, stylish person with coiffed white hair and a wardrobe of sleek suits. She thought the dentist sounded shy and that Jill should encourage him to, as she put it, 'come out and play.'

'But something about him feels off,' said Jill. 'Like maybe he's a pervert of some kind.'

'Why do you interpret his behavior as in some way perverted?'

'Because . . . well, I don't think it's conscious. But it's like he's being apparently nice to me, and then when I respond he pulls away. Only it's more complicated. First he seems like one thing, and then like the other.' She paused. 'I can't explain it. I just feel it. There's something funny going on.'

The therapist said that 'in the culture,' many people had

not been confirmed enough so that they could extend themselves to other people with 'the full capacity of their being,' because 'the culture' was in a state of spiritual lassitude that enforced a level of blandness as the only acceptable way of relating. Underneath, she continued, was a great longing for free, unconvoluted expression, in which beings could be fully present with one another. She thought Jill's dream was about this desire in herself, that the man on the path was her unintegrated male side, who was providing her with an opportunity to 'take the initiative' and thus integrate her maleness. Why not just call him, she suggested, and tell him she would be delighted to get to know him in an unguarded way?

Jill liked the sound of this, although she wasn't sure it had anything to do with the dentist. She discussed it further with her friend Doreen.

'I don't know,' said Doreen. 'He just sounds like a prick to me.'

'Why? I mean, an actual prick?'

'Look, he's fucking with your mind. He does all this stuff for you, which usually would mean he wants to do it with you, and when you get interested he's not there. "Feed the dog"? What's that? All this crap about saying he'll call and then he doesn't? I'd say your instincts are right on.'

Doreen was a former backup singer Jill had met through Joshua. She was forty-two. She lived in a tiny basement room in a house that she shared with several people, all of whom were on minimal government support for ex-drug addicts. The house was an odd mix of squalor, comfort, and mundane beauty. In the small, sorry yard giant roses grew, the petals almost fleshy in their dense unfolding, swollen with failing beauty. Adults, children, and animals lived together in the house, all scrambling after their divergent, yet interwoven, lives. The TV was usually on. They ate awful foot and snacked hideously from pails of discount ice cream and bowls of candy. Doreen thought one of the little girls was being molested in day care, but the mother, who suspected Doreen of secret drug use and was trying to get her thrown out of the house, thought Doreen was dramatizing.

Doreen kept to herself in the basement, where she could smoke. She had covered the walls with paintings depicting horrible scenes from her childhood and posters of rock stars. Every time they talked, Doreen told the same stories about her abusive mother and her experiences with bands and coke dealers. They talked of other things too, but variations of these stories always ran through the weave. Jill had heard them many times, but she still liked the way Doreen told them: as sad and absurd as they were, she brought them out as if they were exquisite silk prints that she fluttered before Jill's eyes and then lovingly folded away. It was as if, in preserving and keeping the stories present, she was somehow preserving herself even though the stories were often about situations that had hurt her and led to her decline. Doreen was sick with hepatitis C, which would probably kill her one day. Even in this state her face had a strong, bitter beauty. Her full lips were well defined and richly striated, so that they resembled thick, fleshy petals. When she listened to Jill, she kept her lips open in a tense oval, which made her look dramatically receptive.

Doreen thought the dentist sounded like a speed freak exboyfriend of hers, who had cruelly manipulated her and stolen drugs from her besides. Jill thought it was an odd comparison. But as she sat there amid Doreen's paintings, watching her put her cigarette between her dry, beautifully striated lips, she imagined the strange, staring night face she had given the dentist, his actual stilted calm, his jovial, seducing phone voice,

The Dentist

all in contrast to Doreen's wounded, still-potent femaleness. Again, she thought of the killer and the weeping mother who willfully drew near him.

Which made no sense, she thought. Surely the dentist was not a killer. She walked up the steep hill to her apartment, the cool wind making her dried sweat feel matte and almost grainy on her skin. It was night, and the slim branches of flower bushes swayed against the city light of the sky, their silhouettes trembling eerily. She remembered the dentist at his office with his hands in her mouth. She was aroused, and the ridiculousness of her arousal embarrassed her. But that wasn't the dentist's fault, was it?

During the next two weeks she called him twice. He seemed delighted to hear from her. He asked her how 'that tooth' was doing. He talked about his work. His tone was jolly and defeated, as if Jill naturally understood – as if anybody would understand – that defeat and boredom were inevitable, and there was something jolly and comforting about that. Jill told him about the masochistic performance artist, how he had suffered as a child and how that had informed his masochism. The dentist seemed interested. He said he liked 'freak shows,' the old-style carnival ones. 'A good geek is hard to find,' he said. Jill said that she didn't think this particular masochist was about a geek thing.

'He encourages people to relate to him,' she said, 'to see how his masochism is just a different way of dealing with pain that everybody has.'

'Yeah, well, I –'

'I mean, look at the flap about recovered memories of sex abuse,' she chattered. 'As a subject, sex abuse had become a metaphor for a lot of different kinds of pain. The problem is –'

'But sex abuse isn't a metaphor, it's –'

'What I mean is, I think many people with these recovered memories are really describing psychic abuse when they say they were molested, only they don't have the language to describe that even to themselves. Lots and lots of people have experienced some severe neglect or emotional disregard as children. So when their therapists give them these suggestions of sexual violation, it rings true to them. Even though they may not have been literally violated.'

'But that's shit,' blurted the dentist. 'Families are being destroyed over these accusations, because somebody thinks they didn't get enough attention when they were five?'

Excited by this thrilling friction, Jill shoved forward. 'I don't know how you were raised, George. But in this culture, in lots of families the level of emotional vibrancy is so low and so bland, and there's so much emphasis on conformity –'

'I hate it when people talk about this culture as if it's worse than anywhere else,' he said.

'Well, maybe other places are like that too; I don't know. I'm just saying that for really bright, open kids, that denial of depth and intensity – it's like having their arms and legs chopped off. It *is* violent. Besides, a lot of people are literally molested, and a lot of them do forget it.'

'But they've done studies that show that kids almost never forget traumatic experiences. The more traumatic and painful it is, the more likely you'll remember it.'

'Well, *I* was molested when I was five and I forgot it. I remembered it when I was ten, when I was watching some old cartoons with bad animation, where the lips on the characters moved really stiff and disconnectedly from the rest of the face. I think it was because when the guy molested me, he didn't look at me while he was doing it – he kept talking about other subjects, like nothing was happening. So when I saw those

The Dentist

weird, jerking lips I got so excited I had to go masturbate, and while I was masturbating, I remembered being molested.'

There was silence on the other end of the phone. Jill had the distinct sense that the dentist had not liked hearing about her masturbating as a child but didn't feel he could say so. She felt him move away. She moved forward.

'So,' she said, 'I think the reason those cartoons made me remember was that the guy who molested me – his mouth and eyes were totally stiff and disconnected.' She did not tell him how she had felt before she got up to masturbate, of her embarrassment, her terrible sense of vulnerability, her feeling that everyone in the room – her brother, her sister, her father – could see what she was feeling. She did not tell him that after she had finished masturbating, her embarrassment became shame, and that the shame was so intense that she had gone to hide in her parents' closet, way in the back, under her mother's coat, where she held herself tight and tried to breathe.

Silence.

'George?' she said. 'Does it make you uncomfortable that I'm talking like this?'

He said no, she could talk about whatever she wanted, but he had to go now. He said he would call her, except that he might be too busy.

Jill hung up feeling a little funny that she'd talked about being molested and the resultant masturbation. But she had wanted so badly for him to see what she'd meant. Since people talked about sex abuse all the time anyway, she had thought it was okay. But in retrospect, she thought, he'd probably just felt the intensity of her want pressing upon him without knowing what it was about, while being forced to think about her genitals. It must've been pretty confusing.

Late that night, she was startled awake by sounds that she thought might've been made by someone coming in the window. The first thought that followed her fear was that the intruder was the dentist, but there wasn't anyone there at all. She lay back in bed and breathed deeply to slow her heart. It occurred to her that her feelings about the dentist were like the feelings she'd had when she'd seen those cheap, poorly done cartoons, that they were the echo of something that was not fully visible to her. Except that while the cartoons had nothing to do with her molestation, she couldn't believe that the dentist's almost morbidly bland public self had nothing to do with the increasingly alarming image she had of him. She felt she was sensing some secret part of him, something that was hurting him as well as her.

She had a lull in writing assignments. She watched TV a lot, mostly shows about crazy middle-aged women who were trying to kill the husbands who had left them for younger women, or shows about crazy perverted men who were trying to kill teenage girls who wouldn't have sex with them. After she was finished watching TV, she sometimes went to bars and drank. She woke in the afternoon with slow, heavy headaches that were almost sweet. She met Joshua for dinner and Doreen for coffee. She talked to Pamela on the phone. At night, the dentist wafted peacefully above her head, close enough to keep her company but too far away for her to beat off about. That was fine with her. When he came into her mind during the day, she regarded him as a friend. She felt they'd gone through a lot together.

It felt very natural for her to call him and leave a message on his answering machine, inviting him to come to her apartment and have a drink. It must've seemed natural for him too,

The Dentist

because he called her back that night, sounding bright and enthusiastic, for him. He said he'd just enjoyed several martinis but that, as usual, 'I don't feel a thing.' She asked him if he'd like to come to her house the following evening and not feel a thing with her – that is, to have a glass of wine after work. He said yes, he'd like that.

When she described the evening to Alex, the magazine editor, she said that she'd grabbed the dentist and reached for his fly, but in truth that never happened; she was just trying to make a good story of it. Alex and she had just cautiously reconciled, after all, and she had wanted to feel close to him. He had started the conversation by telling a story about his unrequited passion for a beautiful young lap dancer, and her lie about the dentist seemed to follow naturally. 'No!' said Alex. 'You didn't!'

'Well, why not?' she replied testily.

'My God, Jill, you probably frightened him to death. Couldn't you have been more gentle?'

She was taken aback; she would've expected a comment like that from Joshua, but Alex was an outrageously self-confident and rather jaded fellow. 'But I wanted him to know how much I liked him,' she said.

'In that case, hold his hand, don't grab his dick.'

'Really? You think?'

'Yes! He probably felt totally unmanned. He sounds like the type who needs to feel in control, and you took that from him.'

It was a nice observation, and probably an apt one even though she'd exaggerated the events of the evening.

They had spent the first hour of their 'drink' in stop-and-start conversation. They talked about Truman Capote and sexual harassment on the street. The dentist expressed outrage at the latter. Jill told him a story about a boy on the street who'd recently grabbed her breast, and how, although she'd turned around and kicked him in the butt, she actually had a certain perverse sympathy for the kid.

'Oh, Jill,' said the dentist, 'you think you're so perverted, but you're really not.'

'I didn't mean perverted, I meant perverse. It's different.'

'Even so. I've seen things you'd never even think of.'

This remark so puzzled her that she disregarded it and raced ahead to describe how she could imagine that if she were a boy and she saw a pair of tits coming down the street, looming out of the dark in a skintight white shirt, she'd probably feel like grabbing one too.

'You mean that was okay with you? Somebody just grabbing your *body*?'

Under the propriety of the words she felt the other thing move. 'George,' she said, 'I've got to ask you something.'

The dentist stood. The expression on his face and his eyes sank inward until nothing showed. 'What?'

She stood too. 'Do you have sexual feelings for me?' she asked.

When she described what had followed to Joshua, she said it was as if they were from different cultures, or that each of them was so involved in projecting onto the other that they weren't actually addressing each other. But it was worse than that.

He said he had never really thought about her sexually. He said he had to spend a lot of time getting to know a person before he had sex. He said this was all very unexpected and he needed to digest it. He asked if she would like to see a movie with him next week. She understood his words. She understood the sentiments that would seem, at least, to lie behind his words. But she felt something beneath those words that she didn't understand. She said she didn't want to see a movie. She said that if they got to know each other, they probably wouldn't want to have sex. She told him that if she'd waited to get to know people before having sex, she'd probably still be a virgin. She didn't understand what moved beneath her own words. It seemed too big to be chipped off in word form, but it didn't matter; she kept talking until the dentist stepped forward and embraced her. She closed her eyes and extended her face upward, to kiss him. There was no sexual feeling in her body, and she didn't feel any in his. That made her want to press against him all the more fiercely, as if she were pinching numb flesh to feel the dull satisfaction of force without effect. Then he bent his head and kissed her on the lips. She glimpsed his face; it was infused with tentative lewdness. A thin shock of sexual feeling flew up her center. It scared her as much as if it had been a tongue of flame shooting out of thin air, and she stepped away as quickly as he did. She almost said, 'George, I'm scared, I'm so scared.' But she didn't.

'I've gotta go,' he said.

'Wait a minute,' she said. She put her hands on his shoulders and pushed him down on the couch, except the pressure she exerted wasn't enough to properly be called a push. Even so he sat, with a little affectation of imbalance; a sensualized shadow of benevolent goofiness passed over his face. It was familiar and dear, this shadow, and she couldn't have it. In truth, she probably didn't even want it, and he probably knew that. It occurred to her that he couldn't have it, either, even though 'it' was him. She sat down and curled her body against his. He put his arms around her.

'Do you think this is strange?' she asked.

'Am I supposed to think it's strange?'

'I don't know. *I* think it's strange.'

'Why?'

'Because you're not my type at all.'

'Then why . . . ?'

'I don't know.' Her voice was as false and cute as that of a ventriloquist's dummy. But her real voice wouldn't come out. She put her head against his chest. He stroked her hair. He said, 'I have to go, Jill. I have to feed the dog. I'll call you. I know I always say that, but I will this time.'

On his way out, he complimented her on her choice of wine.

She boiled some asparagus, poured salt on it, ate it, and watched TV. She watched a show about a crazy middle-aged woman who seduced teenage boys and then made them kill people. About halfway through it, it occurred to her that the dentist was her type after all.

She didn't think of him that night. But in the nights that followed, she did. In her thoughts they did not have sex. They did not talk or look at each other. He only touched her in order to pierce her genitals with needles. She did not look at him or talk to him or touch him.

Jill described these thoughts to her therapist. She said she wouldn't consider them problematic if the dentist had been willing to put them into practice with her, but that it had become increasingly clear that he was not. She asked the therapist why she had encouraged her to be friendly with the dentist, pointing out that everyone else she knew had warned her off him. The therapist said that what Jill had described sounded like a fairly typical man who was perhaps a little bit frightened and immature, and that she thought Jill's friends were simply 'speaking out of their defenses.' Jill said that even if that were true, it was clear that her attraction had devolved into a masochistic compulsion and that the dentist himself appeared to be in the grip of some ghastly, half-conscious sadism. The therapist said that just because Jill had been hurt by the dentist didn't make him a sadist, and Jill conceded that this was true.

'The thing is, I didn't want it to be about a piercing fantasy,' she said. 'And I don't think he wanted it to be this way, either. So I don't understand what happened.'

By the end of the session, it was decided that Jill projected her fears onto the dentist and then judged him, and that the more she judged, the more fear she felt. 'I'd like to encourage you to stop taking a victim stance,' said the therapist. 'Why don't you show some compassion?'

Pamela thought the therapist sounded like an idiot. She thought that the dentist was a secret sadist; even Joshua, who still maintained that the dentist was just 'a scared guy,' thought he'd acted like a jerk. Doreen said he reminded her of a guy who had raped her some years back. Jill reminded her that the dentist felt he didn't know her well enough to rape her.

'Well, this guy didn't technically rape me, either,' said Doreen. 'It was more of a head trip. He was like a poodle on my leg for months, even following me into my house to bug me. So finally, the last time he did that, I said, "Look, I don't give a shit. You want it so bad, you can have it. Just do it and then get the fuck out of my life." And I took my pants off and just lay on the bed. I thought he'd be too embarrassed to do it, but he wasn't. He fucked me.'

'Did he at least get lost after that?'

'Yeah.' Doreen laughed and blew smoke. 'That was the good part.'

She decided to write the dentist a note. She wrote that she was very confused about what had happened between them.

She wrote that she had deeply appreciated the respect and kindness he had shown at the beginning of their relationship and that she didn't understand why he now disrespected her by not calling her when he said he would. If he wanted to break off contact, she understood, but she would prefer him to do so in a spirit of kindness. She went to his office and left the note with his secretary, who smiled at her conspiratorially.

'He actually called about the note,' she said to Lila. 'He seemed like he really wanted to talk. His voice sounded different and everything.'

'Yeah?' Briskly, Lila wrapped a piece of cellophane around Jill's chemical-treated hair. 'How was his voice different?'

'More feeling. Softer.' Like he was having the pleasure of an emotional experience that would cost him nothing. 'He said he had just been sorry that the tooth experience turned out so badly and that's why he loaned me the computer. He apologized for not communicating and said he wasn't very emotionally connected but that he liked me a lot. I said, Well, do you want to fuck or not?'

'Hah!'

'I guess it was kind of obnoxious. Anyway, he said, no, he didn't think so. He said he couldn't do it just like that. He said he was from the Midwest and that they were gentlemen there. He said he had to go but that he'd call me, which of course he didn't.'

'You should've told him that gentlemen call ladies when they say they will.'

'Yeah, and anyway, what does he mean, that he's too much of a gentleman to do it with me?'

'Oh, no, I doubt it. Men are just funny. You remember that

Italian guy I was with? I had a totally different situation with him. It was almost all sex right from the beginning.'

'Was it nice?'

'It was . . . gymnastic. And it was nice for a while, but then I began to feel like he was treating me like a whore. So I told him that. And he said, You know, you're right.' Lila nodded with a satisfied equanimity that was augmented by the smart, nimble movements of her working fingers. 'That was pretty much the end of the relationship, which was too bad in a way. We actually liked each other a lot. But the sex thing just went over the top.'

They were silent while Lila attended to Jill's hair. Jill enjoyed being enveloped in women's voices and canned music and hair dryer noise. She loved being in a room of women engaged in personal bodily rituals meant to fulfill the need for understandable public signals. The women who worked here had a slightly beat-up, stalwart air, and there was a gallantry to their little pieces of jewelry, their inexpensive but smartly belted and accessorized outfits, their fussy fingernails, the jiggling curls one wore on either side of her face.

'Lila, you used to be in Sex and Love Addicts Anonymous, right?'

'Yeah, for a year and a half. Why?'

'My therapist suggested it. She said they make you promise to not have sex with anybody until you've known them for six months. But I don't see how that would help. If you're going to be compulsive, it seems like you could easily drag your compulsion out for six months. I know *I* could.'

'Yeah, well, frankly, I came to the same conclusion.' With a graceful slouch, Lila reached for the cup of coffee amid her implements. 'Although I also saw people do a lot of growing and sharing.'

★

The last time Jill saw the dentist, she went to his office. She went when she knew he would just be finishing his office hours. She expected the secretary to be there, but she wasn't. When Jill saw her empty desk, she hesitated. A door opened and the dentist emerged. He looked at her with the same neutral calm he had worn when he was tearing her tooth out piece by piece.

'Hi,' said Jill. 'I was in the neighborhood and I thought I'd drop by.'

He said he was glad to see her but that the automatic surveillance system was just about to go on, and if anyone was in the room besides him, it would arouse the hired security.

'That's okay,' she said. 'I just dropped by on my way to an early movie.'

'Oh?' He sounded curious. 'What are you seeing?'

'Just some silly thing this friend of mine's ex-wife is in. She wouldn't have sex with him for a year before they got divorced, and in the movie she's playing opposite her new girlfriend, who in the movie apparently fucks the shit out of her with a strap-on. You'd think her ex-husband would be jealous, but I guess he's just so proud of her for getting the part.'

'Well, like I said, the system's about to go on.'

'Yeah, okay. I just wanted to ask you something.' She got distracted by the cup of cold coffee on the secretary's desk, its red lipstick impress weak and melancholy in the harsh office light. The dentist followed her eye, and they both stared at the cup. 'The last time you were at my house, why did you say I thought I was so perverted, when I'm really not?'

'I don't remember saying that.'

'You did. You said you'd seen things I couldn't even imagine, and I just wondered –'

'I don't remember, but I'm sure it didn't mean anything.'

The Dentist

He removed his white coat with such agitation he got his wrist stuck in one sleeve.

'But people usually mean –'

'I don't *mean* anything! I'm a very simple person! I'm bland and I have a low level of emotional vibrancy and I like it that way!' He wrested his wrist free, then frantically fooled with his tie.

'But –'

'Why are you always saying these strange things to me? What do you want? Why are you always talking about sex?'

'I'm not talking about sex right now. I –'

'I didn't say you were! But you – you're – I'm just trying to be –'

To her grief, she saw it was true: he was apoplectic with fear.

Oh, honey, she thought. Oh, darling.

'Call me tomorrow,' he said thickly. 'I can't talk anymore now.'

This incident made a very funny story. Everyone laughed when Jill told it a few nights later, at a dinner with Alex the magazine editor, his friend the television producer, and an assortment of writers eager for a free dinner and an assignment. Most of the people at the table knew each other only tangentially; they had been assembled through an acquaintance of the producer's, on the grounds that they were the most interesting people in San Francisco.

'So at that point I was, like, this guy is kooky, so I just said goodbye and went to leave. And so he *follows me out* and holds the door for me and says, "Sorry I had to kick you out. But the rules are the rules." Referring, I suppose, to the automatic surveillance system.'

'He really does sound peculiar,' said Alex.

Alex and the television producer had come from New

York on business. Most of the writers present were also 'sex workers,' although one of them, an earnest bald woman, handed out cards advertising a therapy by which to recover from sex abuse. The television producer, a melancholy person with whom Jill once had a minor telephone flirtation, confided in her that Alex had arranged this dinner in order to meet Cindy, a determined and impish woman who published a stylish sex magazine. She had apparently written an article about anal sex which had gotten under his skin and provoked a correspondence. She seemed very nice, but Jill wondered why Alex couldn't find anyone to have anal sex with in New York.

'Why do you like this guy?' Cindy asked. 'Is he sexy in any way?'

'Not in the normal ways.' Jill imagined the dentist standing before these people, and the bewildered looks on their faces. 'Except I could feel . . . I'm convinced he's a secret pervert and that he just doesn't know it yet.'

Cindy smiled appreciatively. 'You think if you could just get him into a sling, he'd be fine?'

'No, I don't think he'd ever actually get into a sling, whether he wanted to or not. I think he'd just keep getting into sling-like positions in inappropriate situations.' Jill had of course just described herself, but Cindy didn't know that, so she laughed. Jill wondered how Cindy would've reacted if she'd said, 'Because I thought he was kind.'

Several of the guests began to discuss the politics of the various strip clubs around town, one of them denouncing 'those corporate strippers' who were really just middle-class girls who thought it was cool to be a sex worker. Someone else expressed disdain for those who said sex workers had all suffered child abuse and did such work as a result. Another got irritated over the negative portrayals of sex workers in the media. The woman to Jill's left was muttering darkly about her desire to infect the water supply with chemicals that would sterilize the population.

Longingly, Jill thought of the dentist at home with his entertainment center. As if reading her mind, Alex said she should've invited the dentist to the dinner this evening. 'He wouldn't have come, of course. He would've driven up and down the street looking in the windows over and over again, wondering whether or not he should come in. It would've driven him crazy.'

'I don't want to drive him crazy,' said Jill. 'He's shy, Alex.'

'Nonsense. Of course you want to drive him crazy. And in the long run you will. Because you touched his fear. Every time he sees anything you've written, he'll think of you and twist a bit.'

'You think?'

'Oh, yes. Why do you think I put out a magazine? So that girls I've been with will see it and twist.' Alex's voice as he said this was calm, but underneath was a muffled agitation that made Jill think of the dentist wresting his wrist out of his sleeve. It made Jill want to hold Alex and stroke his head. 'I wanted him to pierce my genitals with needles,' she said dreamily. 'It's funny. That's not something I usually fantasize about.'

'Was he wearing his white coat while he pierced you?'

'No. He was just George.' George with his glassy eyes, his cold lips, his jocular warmth held far away in a tiny place.

'That's the trouble with your fantasies,' said Alex. 'You haven't got the right clothes.'

Meanwhile, someone made the argument that it would be awful if the 'mainstream' ever came to truly accept whatever anybody might want to do sexually, because then sex wouldn't be shocking anymore.

'That won't ever happen,' said Jill. 'Sex is too complicated, it means too many things to people. It connects to the dirt within, and there's just too much dirt.'

'You're wrong,' said the television producer. 'It's already happened, in San Francisco anyway.'

Their words were such announcements, yet Jill could barely feel the life in them. She tried to fixate on the dentist, but he only came to her in faint, cold wisps of idea. The woman next to her was describing a transvestite bar to which they might go after dinner. She said that when loathsome suburban men came to her strip shows expecting to buy sex, she sent them to this place as a joke, archly informing them that 'the ladies' there would be pleased 'to negotiate.' She was tall and full of disdain. Her long black hair was dull and fake, her eyes were made up huge and dark in her chalky face, her lips were full and dry; like a starved feral cat, she appeared both fierce and desperately unctuous, which was interesting with her disdainful affect. Jill thought she was beautiful and wanted to talk to her, but the woman's words were harsh and so full of puzzling judgments that Jill was afraid of her. She looked down at the woman's hands, which were delicate and looked strangely lost in their movements, the nails pathetically small and bitten. Jill put her own hand down on the table so that their wrists were touching. The woman let her wrist stay there, and Jill thought she could feel her through her skin. She did not feel harsh or disdainful; she felt like a tense animal, very fearful but also resourceful and curious, even rather innocent. Jill thought she could feel the woman sensing her back, as one animal sniffs another. But then she moved her hand.

Jill and Alex left at the same time. They stood on the street for some moments, chatting. He said that he had gone to a sex store to get toys in anticipation of his tryst with Cindy. He said he was going to tie her up, and he pulled a piece of black thong from his pocket, apparently thinking that Jill would want to see it. Jill thought that if she hugged him goodbye, it might generate feelings of warmth and friendship, but it only made her feel uncomfortable.

'I'm enjoying your discomfort,' he said.

'I'm glad someone is,' she answered.

They kissed each other goodbye. Alex got into a cab and sped away. As the evening was warm and mild, Jill decided to walk a little. Homeless people strolled about, pushing shopping carts full of hoarded things. Traffic ran and darted according to plan. She imagined the dentist driving up and down the street, staring at the restaurant, trying to glimpse the dinner party inside. She imagined his eyes moving back and forth as he turned his head away from the window and then looked back again. She was distracted by the sound of someone muttering. It was a man crouching on the sidewalk in dirty, wadded blankets. He glared at her. 'If it's a man, I'll castrate him and stuff his balls in his mouth,' he said. 'If it's a woman, I'll stick my fist up her cunt and fuck her dead.' Jill understood how he felt, but she still walked a few feet up before she stepped off the curb to hail a cab.

Secretary

The typing and secretarial class was held in a little basement room in the Business Building of the local community college. The teacher was an old lady with hair that floated in vague clouds around her temples and Kleenex stuck up the sleeve of her dress for some future, probably nasal purpose. She held a stopwatch in one old hand and tilted her hip as she watched us all with severe, imperial eyes, not caring that her stomach hung out. The girl in front of me had short, clenched blond curls sitting on her thin shoulders. Lone strands would stick straight out from her head in cold, dry weather.

It was a two-hour class with a ten-minute break. Everybody would go out in the hall during the break to get coffee or candy from the machines. The girls would stand in groups and talk, and the two male typists would walk slowly up and down the corridor with round shoulders, holding their Styrofoam cups and looking into the bright slits of light in the business class doors as they passed by.

I would go to the big picture window that looked out onto the parking lot and stare at the streetlights shining on the hoods of the cars.

After class, I'd come home and put my books on the dining room table among the leftover dinner things: balled-up napkins, glasses of water, a dish of green beans sitting on a pot holder. My father's plate would always be there, with gnawed bones and hot pepper on it. He would be in the living room

Secretary

in his pajama top with a dish of ice cream in his lap and his hair on end. 'How many words a minute did you type tonight?' he'd ask.

It wasn't an unreasonable question, but the predictable and agitated delivery of it was annoying. It reflected his way of hoarding silly details and his obsessive fear I would meet my sister's fate. She'd had a job at a home for retarded people for the past eight years. She wore jeans and a long army coat to work every day. When she came home, she went up to her room and lay in bed. Every now and then she would come down and joke around or watch TV, but not much.

Mother would drive me around to look for jobs. First we would go through ads in the paper, drawing black circles, marking X's. The defaced newspaper sat on the dining room table in a gray folder and we argued.

'I'm not friendly and I'm not personable. I'm not going to answer an ad for somebody like that. It would be stupid.'

'You can be friendly. And you are personable when you aren't busy putting yourself down.'

'I'm not putting myself down. You just want to think that I am so you can have something to talk about.'

'You're backing yourself into a corner, Debby.'

'Oh, shit.' I picked up a candy wrapper and began pinching it together in an ugly way. My hands were red and rough. It didn't matter how much lotion I used.

'Come on, we're getting started on the wrong foot.'

'Shut up.'

My mother crossed her legs. 'Well,' she said. She picked up the 'Living' section of the paper and cracked it into position. She tilted her head back and dropped her eyelids. Her upper lip became hostile as she read. She picked up her green teacup and drank.

'I'm dependable. I could answer an ad for somebody dependable.'

'You are that.'

We wound up in the car. My toes swelled in my high heels. My mother and I both used the flowered box of Kleenex on the dashboard and stuck the used tissue in a brown bag that sat near the hump in the middle of the car. There was a lot of traffic in both lanes. We drove past the Amy Joy doughnut shop. They still hadn't put the letter Y back on the Amy sign.

Our first stop was Wonderland. There was a job in the clerical department of Sears. The man there had a long disapproving nose, and he held his hands stiffly curled in the middle of his desk. He mainly looked at his hands. He said he would call me, but I knew he wouldn't.

On the way back to the parking lot, we passed a pet store. There were only hamsters, fish and exhausted yellow birds. We stopped and looked at slivers of fish swarming in their tank of thick green water. I had come to this pet store when I was ten years old. The mall had just opened and we had all come out to walk through it. My sister, Donna, had wanted to go into the pet store. It was very warm and damp in the store, and smelled like fur and hamster. When we walked out, it seemed cold. I said I was cold and Donna took off her white leatherette jacket and put it around my shoulders, letting one hand sit on my left shoulder for a minute. She had never touched me like that before and she hasn't since.

The next place was a tax information office in a slab of building with green trim. They gave me an intelligence test that was mostly spelling and 'What's wrong with this sentence?' The woman came out of her office holding my test and smiling. 'You scored higher than anyone else I've interviewed,' she said. 'You're really overqualified for this job. There's no challenge. You'd be bored to death.'

'I want to be bored,' I said.

She laughed. 'Oh, I don't think that's true.'

We had a nice talk about what people want out of their jobs and then I left.

'Well, I hope you weren't surprised that you had the highest score,' said my mother.

We went to the French bakery on Eight-Mile Road and got cookies called elephant ears. We ate them out of a bag as we drove. I felt so comfortable, I could have driven around in the car all day.

Then we went to a lawyer's office on Telegraph Road. It was a receding building made of orange brick. There were no other houses or stores around it, just a parking lot and some taut fir trees that looked like they had been brushed. My mother waited for me in the car. She smiled, took out a crossword puzzle and focused her eyes on it, the smile still gripping her face.

The lawyer was a short man with dark, shiny eyes and dense immobile shoulders. He took my hand with an indifferent aggressive snatch. It felt like he could have put his hand through my rib cage, grabbed my heart, squeezed it a little to see how it felt, then let go. 'Come into my office,' he said.

We sat down and he fixed his eyes on me. 'It's not much of a job,' he said. 'I have a paralegal who does research and leg-work, and the proofreading gets done at an agency. All I need is a presentable typist who can get to work on time and answer the phone.'

'I can do that,' I said.

'It's very dull work,' he said.

'I like dull work.'

He stared at me, his eyes becoming hooded in thought. 'There's something about you,' he said. 'You're closed up, you're tight. You're like a wall.'

'I know.'

My answer surprised him and his eyes lost their hoods. He tilted his head back and looked at me, his shiny eyes bared again. 'Do you ever loosen up?'

The corners of my mouth jerked, smilelike. 'I don't know.' My palms sweated.

His secretary, who was leaving, called me the next day and said that he wanted to hire me. Her voice was serene, flat and utterly devoid of inflection.

'That typing course really paid off,' said my father. 'You made a good investment.' He wandered in and out of the dining room in pleased agitation, holding his glass of beer. 'A law office could be a fascinating place.' He arched his chin and scratched his throat.

Donna even came downstairs and made popcorn and put it in a big yellow bowl on the table for everybody to eat. She ate lazily, her large hand dawdling in the bowl. 'It could be okay. Interesting people could come in. Even though that lawyer's probably an asshole.'

My mother sat quietly, pleased with her role in the job-finding project, pinching clusters of popcorn in her fingers and popping them into her mouth.

That night I put my new work clothes on a chair and looked at them. A brown skirt, a beige blouse. I was attracted to the bland ugliness, but I didn't know how long that would last. I looked at their gray shapes in the night-light and then rolled over toward the dark corner of my bed.

My family's enthusiasm made me feel sarcastic about the

job – about any effort to do anything, in fact. In light of their enthusiasm, the only intelligent course of action seemed to be immobility and rudeness. But in the morning, as I ate my poached eggs and toast, I couldn't help but feel curious and excited. The feeling grew as I rode in the car with my mother to the receding orange building. I felt like I was accomplishing something. I wanted to do well. When we drove past the Amy Joy doughnut shop, I saw, through a wall of glass, expectant construction workers in heavy boots and jackets sitting on vinyl swivel seats, waiting for coffee and bags of doughnuts. I had sentimental thoughts about workers and the decency of unthinking toil. I was pleased to be like them, insofar as I was. I returned my mother's smile when I got out of the car and said 'thanks' when she said 'good luck.'

'Well, here you are,' said the lawyer. He clapped his short, hard-packed little hands together and made a loud noise. 'On time. Good morning!'

He began training me then and continued to do so all week. No interesting people came into the office. Very few people came into the office at all. The first week there were three. One was a nervous middle-aged woman who had an uneven haircut and was wearing lavender rubber children's boots. She sat on the edge of the waiting room chair with her rubber boots together, rearranging the things in her purse. Another was a fat woman in a bright, baglike dress who had yellow in the whites of her wild little eyes, and who carried her purse like a weapon. The last was a man who sat desperately turning his head as if he wanted to disconnect it from his body. I could hear him raising his voice inside the lawyer's office. When he left, the lawyer came out and said, 'He is completely crazy,' and told me to type him a bill for five hundred dollars.

Everyone who sat in the waiting room looked random and

unwelcome. They all fidgeted. The elegant old armchairs and puffy upholstered couch were themselves disoriented in the stiff modernity of the waiting room. My heavy oak desk was an idiot standing against a wall covered with beige plaster. The brooding plants before me gave the appearance of weighing a lot for plants, even though one of them was a slight, frondy thing.

I was surprised that a person like the lawyer, who seemed to be mentally organized and evenly distributed, would have such an office. But I was comfortable in it. Its jumbled nature was like a nest of available rags gathered tightly together for warmth. My first two weeks were serene. I enjoyed the dullness of days, the repetition of motions, the terms, polite interactions between the lawyer and me. I enjoyed feeling him impose his brainlessly confident sense of existence on me. He would say, 'Type this letter,' and my sensibility would contract until the abstractions of achievement and production found expression in the typing of the letter. I was useful.

My mother picked me up every day. We would usually stop at the A&P before we went home to get a loaf of white French bread, beer and kielbasa sausage for my father. When we got home I would go upstairs to my room, take off my skirt and blouse, and throw them on the floor. I would get into my bed of jumbled blankets in my underwear and panty hose and listen to my father yelling at my mother until I fell asleep. I woke up when Donna pounded on my door and yelled, 'Dinner!'

I would go down with her then and sit at the table. We would all watch the news on TV as we ate. My mother would have a shrunken, abstracted look on her face. My father would hunch over his plate like an animal at its dish.

After dinner, I would go upstairs and listen to records and write in my diary or play Parcheesi with Donna until it was time to get ready for bed. I'd go to sleep at night looking at the skirt and blouse I would wear the next day. I'd wake up looking at my ceramic weather poodle, which was supposed to turn pink, blue or green, depending on the weather, but had only turned gray and stayed gray. I would hear my father in the bathroom, the tumble of radio patter, the water, the clink of a glass being set down, the creak and click as he closed the medicine cabinet. Donna would be standing outside my door, waiting for him to finish, muttering 'shit' or something.

Looking back on it, I don't know why that time was such a contented one, but it was.

The first day of the third week, the lawyer came out of his office, stiffer than usual, his eyes lit up in a peculiar, stalking way. He was carrying one of my letters. He put it on my desk, right in front of me. 'Look at it,' he said. I did.

'Do you see that?'

'What?' I asked.

'This letter has three typing errors in it, one of which is, I think, a spelling error.'

'I'm sorry.'

'This isn't the first time either. There have been others that I let go because it was your first few weeks. But this can't go on. Do you know what this makes me look like to the people who receive these letters?'

I looked at him, mortified. There had been a catastrophe hidden in the folds of my contentment for two weeks and he hadn't even told me. It seemed unfair, although when I thought about it I could understand his reluctance, maybe even embarrassment, to draw my attention to something so stupidly unpleasant.

'Type it again.'

I did, but I was so badly shaken that I made even more

mistakes. 'You are wasting my time,' he said, and handed it to me once again. I typed it correctly the third time, but he sulked in his office for the rest of the day.

This kind of thing kept occurring all week. Each time, the lawyer's irritation and disbelief mounted. In addition, I sensed something else growing in him, an intimate tendril creeping from one of his darker areas, nursed on the feeling that he had discovered something about me.

I was very depressed about the situation. When I went home in the evening I couldn't take a nap. I lay there looking at the gray weather poodle and fantasized about having a conversation with the lawyer that would clear up everything, explain to him that I was really trying to do my best. He seemed to think that I was making the mistakes on purpose.

At the end of the week he began complaining about the way I answered the phone. 'You're like a machine,' he said. 'You sound like you're in the Twilight Zone. You don't think when you respond to people.'

When he asked me to come into his office at the end of the day, I thought he was going to fire me. The idea was a relief, but a numbing one. I sat down and he fixed me with a look that was speculative but benign, for him. He leaned back in his chair in a comfortable way, one hand dangling sideways from his wrist. To my surprise, he began talking to me about my problems, as he saw them.

'I sense that you are a very nice but complex person, with wild mood swings that you keep hidden. You just shut up the house and act like there's nobody home.'

'That's true,' I said. 'I do that.'

'Well, why? Why don't you open up a little bit? It would probably help your typing.'

It was really not any of his business, I thought.

Secretary

'You should try to talk more. I know I'm your employer and we have a prescribed relationship, but you should feel free to discuss your problems with me.'

The idea of discussing my problems with him was preposterous. 'It's hard to think of having that kind of discussion with you,' I said. I hesitated. 'You have a strong personality and . . . when I encounter a personality like that, I tend to step back because I don't know how to deal with it.'

He was clearly pleased with this response, but he said, 'You shouldn't be so shy.'

When I thought about this conversation later, it seemed, on the one hand, that this lawyer was just an asshole. On the other, his comments were weirdly moving, and had the effect of making me feel horribly sensitive. No one had ever made such personal comments to me before.

The next day I made another mistake. The intimacy of the previous day seemed to make the mistake even more repulsive to him because he got madder than usual. I wanted him to fire me. I would have suggested it, but I was struck silent. I sat and stared at the letter while he yelled. 'What's wrong with you!'

'I'm sorry,' I said.

He stood quietly for a moment. Then he said, 'Come into my office. And bring that letter.'

I followed him into his office.

'Put that letter on my desk,' he said.

I did.

'Now bend over so that you are looking directly at it. Put your elbows on the desk and your face very close to the letter.'

Shaken and puzzled, I did what he said.

'Now read the letter to yourself. Keep reading it over and over again.'

I read: 'Dear Mr Garvy: I am very grateful to you for referring . . .' He began spanking me as I said 'referring.' The funny thing was, I wasn't even surprised. I actually kept reading the letter, although my understanding of it was not very clear. I began crying on it, which blurred the ink. The word 'humiliation' came into my mind with such force that it effectively blocked out all other words. Further, I felt that the concept it stood for had actually been a major force in my life for quite a while.

He spanked me for about ten minutes, I think. I read the letter only about five times, partly because it rapidly became too wet to be legible. When he stopped he said, 'Now straighten up and go type it again.'

I went to my desk. He closed the office door behind him. I sat down, blew my nose and wiped my face. I stared into space for several minutes, every now and then dwelling on the tingling sensation in my buttocks. I typed the letter again and took it into his office. He didn't look up as I put it on his desk.

I went back out and sat, planning to sink into a stupor of some sort. But a client came in, so I couldn't. I had to buzz the lawyer and tell him the client had arrived. 'Tell him to wait,' he said curtly.

When I told the client to wait, he came up to my desk and began to talk to me. 'I've been here twice before,' he said. 'Do you recognize me?'

'Yes,' I said. 'Of course.' He was a small, tight-looking middle-aged man with agitated little hands and a pale scar running over his lip and down his chin. The scar didn't make him look tough; he was too anxious to look tough.

'I never thought anything like this would ever happen to me,' he said. 'I never thought I'd be in a lawyer's office even once, and I've been here three times now. And absolutely nothing's been accomplished. I've always hated lawyers.' He looked as though he expected me to take offense.

'A lot of people do,' I said.

'It was either that or I would've shot those miserable blankety-blanks next door and I'd have to get a lawyer to defend me anyway. You know the story?'

I did. He was suing his neighbors because they had a dog that 'barked all goddamn day.' I listened to him talk. It surprised me how this short conversation quickly restored my sensibility. Everything seemed perfectly normal by the time the lawyer came out of his office to greet the client. I noticed he had my letter in one hand. Just before he turned to lead the client away, he handed it to me, smiling. 'Good letter,' he said.

When I went home that night, everything was the same. My life had not been disarranged by the event except for a slight increase in the distance between me and my family. My behind was not even red when I looked at it in the bathroom mirror.

But when I got into bed and thought about the thing, I got excited. I was more excited, in fact, than I had ever been in my life. That didn't surprise me, either. I felt a numbness; I felt that I could never have a normal conversation with anyone again. I masturbated slowly, to put off the climax as long as I could. But there was no climax, even though I tried for a long time. Then I couldn't sleep.

It happened twice more in the next week and a half. The following week, when I made a typing mistake, he didn't spank me. Instead, he told me to bend over his desk, look at the typing mistake and repeat 'I am stupid' for several minutes.

Our relationship didn't change otherwise. He was still brisk and friendly in the morning. And, because he seemed so sure of himself, I could not help but react to him as if he were still the same domineering but affable boss. He did not, however, ever invite me to discuss my problems with him again.

I began to have recurring dreams about him. In one, the most frequent, I walked with him in a field of big bright red poppies. The day was brilliant and warm. We were smiling at each other, and there was a tremendous sense of release and goodwill between us. He looked at me and said, 'I understand you now, Debby.' Then we held hands.

There was one time I felt disturbed about what was happening at the office. It was just before dinner, and my father was upset about something that had happened to him at work. I could hear him yelling in the living room while my mother tried to comfort him. He yelled, 'I'd rather work in a circus! In one of those things where you put your head through a hole and people pay to throw garbage at you!'

'No circus has that anymore,' said my mother. 'Stop it, Shep.'

By the time I went down to eat dinner, everything was as usual. I looked at my father and felt a sickening sensation of love nailed to contempt and panic.

The last time I made a typing error and the lawyer summoned me to his office, two unusual things occurred. The first was that after he finished spanking me he told me to pull up my skirt. Fear hooked my stomach and pulled it toward my chest. I turned my head and tried to look at him.

'You're not worried that I'm going to rape you, are you?' he said. 'Don't. I'm not interested in that, not in the least. Pull up your skirt.'

I turned my head away from him. I thought, I don't have to do this. I can stop right now. I can straighten up and walk out. But I didn't. I pulled up my skirt.

'Pull down your panty hose and underwear.'

A finger of nausea poked my stomach.

'I told you I'm not going to fuck you. Do what I say.'

The skin on my face and throat was hot, but my fingertips were cold on my legs as I pulled down my underwear and panty hose. The letter before me became distorted beyond recognition. I thought I might faint or vomit, but I didn't. I was held up by a feeling of dizzying suspension, like the one I have in dreams where I can fly, but only if I get into some weird position.

At first he didn't seem to be doing anything. Then I became aware of a small frenzy of expended energy behind me. I had an impression of a vicious little animal frantically burrowing dirt with its tiny claws and teeth. My hips were sprayed with hot sticky muck.

'Go clean yourself off,' he said. 'And do that letter again.'

I stood slowly, and felt my skirt fall over the sticky gunk. He briskly swung open the door and I left the room, not even pulling up my panty hose and underwear, since I was going to use the bathroom anyway. He closed the door behind me, and the second unusual thing occurred. Susan, the paralegal, was standing in the waiting room with a funny look on her face. She was a blonde who wore short, fuzzy sweaters, and fake gold jewelry around her neck. At her friendliest, she had a whining, abrasive quality that clung to her voice. Now, she could barely say hello. Her stupidly full lips were parted speculatively.

'Hi,' I said. 'Just a minute.' She noted the awkwardness of my walk, because of the lowered panty hose.

I got to the bathroom and wiped myself off. I didn't feel embarrassed. I felt mechanical. I wanted to get that dumb paralegal out of the office so I could come back to the bathroom and masturbate.

Susan completed her errand and left. I masturbated. I retyped the letter. The lawyer sat in his office all day.

When my mother picked me up that afternoon, she asked me if I was all right.

'Why do you ask?'

'I don't know. You look a little strange.'

'I'm as all right as I ever am.'

'That doesn't sound good, honey.'

I didn't answer. My mother moved her hands up and down the steering wheel, squeezing it anxiously.

'Maybe you'd like to stop by the French bakery and get some elephant ears,' she said.

'I don't want any elephant ears.' My voice was unexpectedly nasty. It almost made me cry.

'All right,' said my mother.

When I lay on my bed to take my nap, my body felt dense and heavy, as though it would be very hard to move again, which was just as well, since I didn't feel like moving. When Donna banged on my door and yelled 'Dinner!' I didn't answer. She put her head in and asked if I was asleep, and I told her I didn't feel like eating. I felt so inert, I thought I'd go to sleep, but I couldn't. I lay awake through the sounds of argument and TV and everybody going to the bathroom. Bedtime came, drawers rasped open and shut, doors slammed, my father eased into sleep with radio mumble. The orange digits on my clock said 1:30. I thought: I should get out of this panty hose and slip. I sat up and looked out into the gray, cold street. The shrubbery on the lawn across the street looked frozen and miserable. I thought about the period of time a year before when I couldn't sleep because I kept thinking that someone was going to break into the house and kill everybody. Eventually that fear went away and I went back to sleeping again. I lay back down without taking off my clothes, and pulled a light blanket tightly around me. Sooner or later, I thought, I would sleep. I would just have to wait.

But I didn't sleep, although I became mentally incoherent for long, ugly stretches of time. Hours went by; the room turned gray. I heard the morning noises: the toilet, the coughing, Donna's hostile muttering. Often, in the past, I had woken early and lain in bed listening to my family clumsily trying to organize itself for the day. Often as not, their sounds made me feel irrational loathing. This morning, I felt despair and a longing for them, and a sureness that we would never be close as long as I lived. My nasal passages became active with tears that didn't reach my eyes.

My mother knocked on the door. 'Honey, aren't you going to be late?'

'I'm not going to work. I feel sick. I'll call in.'

'I'll do it for you, just stay in bed.'

'No, I'm going to call. It has to be me.'

I didn't call in. The lawyer didn't call the house. I didn't go in or call the next day or the day after that. The lawyer still didn't call. I was slightly hurt by his absent phone call, but my relief was far greater than my hurt.

After I'd stayed home for four days, my father asked if I wasn't worried about taking so much time off. I told him I'd quit, in front of Donna and my mother. He was dumbfounded.

'That wasn't very smart,' he said. 'What are you going to do now?'

'I don't care,' I said. 'That lawyer was an asshole.' To everyone's discomfort, I began to cry. I left the room, and they all watched me stomp up the stairs.

The next day at dinner my father said, 'Don't get discouraged because your first job didn't work out. There're plenty of other places out there.'

'I don't want to think about another job right now.'

There was a disgruntlement all around the table. 'Come on now, Debby, you don't want to throw away everything you worked for in that typing course,' said my father.

'I don't blame her,' said Donna. 'I'm sick of working for assholes.'

'Oh, shit,' said my father. 'If I had quit every job I've had on those grounds, you would've all starved. Maybe that's what I should've done.'

'What happened, Debby?' said my mother.

I said, 'I don't want to talk about it,' and I left the room again.

After that they may have sensed, with their intuition for the miserable, that something hideous had happened. Because they left the subject alone.

I received my last paycheck from the lawyer in the mail. It came with a letter folded around it. It said, 'I am so sorry for what happened between us. I have realized what a terrible mistake I made with you. I can only hope that you will understand, and that you will not worsen an already unfortunate situation by discussing it with others. All the best.' As a P.S. he assured me that I could count on him for excellent references. He enclosed a check for three hundred and eighty dollars, a little over two hundred dollars more than he owed me.

It occurred to me to tear up the check, or mail it back to the lawyer. But I didn't do that. Two hundred dollars was worth more then than it is now. Together with the money I had in the bank, it was enough to put a down payment on an apartment and still have some left over. I went upstairs and wrote '380' on the deposit side of my checking account. I didn't feel like a whore or anything. I felt I was doing the right thing. I looked at the total figure of my balance with satisfaction. Then I went downstairs and asked my mother if she wanted to go get some elephant ears.

For the next two weeks, I forgot about the idea of a job and moving out of my parents' house. I slept through all the morning noise until noon. I got up and ate cold cereal and ran the dishwasher. I watched the gray march of old sitcoms on TV. I worked on crossword puzzles. I lay on my bed in a tangle of quilt and fuzzy blanket and masturbated two, three, four times in a row, always thinking about the thing.

I was still in this phase when my father stuck the newspaper under my nose and said, 'Did you see what your old boss is doing?' There was a small article on the upcoming mayoral elections in Westland. He was running for mayor. I took the paper from my father's offering hands. For the first time, I felt an uncomplicated disgust for the lawyer. Westland was nothing but malls and doughnut stands and a big ugly theater with an artificial volcano in the front of it. What kind of idiot would want to be mayor of Westland? Again, I left the room.

I got the phone call the next week. It was a man's voice, a soft, probing, condoling voice. 'Miss Roe?' he said. 'I hope you'll forgive this unexpected call. I'm Mark Charming of *Detroit Magazine*.'

I didn't say anything. The voice continued more uncertainly. 'Are you free to talk, Miss Roe?'

There was no one in the kitchen, and my mother was running the vacuum in the next room. 'Talk about what?' I said.

'Your previous employer.' The voice became slightly harsh as he said these words, and then hurriedly rushed back to condolence. 'Please don't be startled or upset. I know this could be a disturbing phone call for you, and it must certainly seem intrusive.' He paused so I could laugh or something. I didn't, and his voice became more cautious. 'The thing is, we're doing a story on your ex-employer in the context of his running for mayor. To put it mildly, we think he has no business running for public office. We think he would be very bad for the whole Detroit area. He has an awful reputation, Miss Roe – which may not surprise you.' There was another careful pause that I did not fill.

'Miss Roe, are you still with me?'

'Yes.'

'What all this is leading up to is that we have reason to believe that you could reveal information about your ex-employer that would be damaging to him. This information would never be connected to your name. We would use a pseudonym. Your privacy would be protected completely.'

The vacuum cleaner shut off, and silence encircled me. My throat constricted.

'Do you want time to think about it, Miss Roe?'

'I can't talk now,' I said, and hung up.

I couldn't go through the living room without my mother asking me who had been on the phone, so I went downstairs to the basement. I sat on the mildewed couch and curled up, unmindful of centipedes. I rested my chin on my knee and stared at the boxes of my father's old paperbacks and the jumble of plastic Barbie-doll cases full of Barbie equipment that Donna and I used to play with on the front porch. A stiff white foot and calf stuck out of a sky-blue case, helpless and pitifully rigid.

For some reason, I remembered the time, a few years before, when my mother had taken me to see a psychiatrist. One of the more obvious questions he had asked me was, 'Debby, do you ever have the sensation of being outside yourself, almost as if you can actually watch yourself from another place?' I hadn't at the time, but I did now. And it wasn't such a bad feeling at all.

Because They Wanted To

Elise sat in the free medical clinic, studying the support group flyers on the bulletin board. There were support groups for gay youths, lesbian youths, bisexual youths, prostitutes and junkies and people who had AIDS. She did not belong in any of those categories, and even if she did, she did not think she would want to go to a support group. But she liked the idea that they were there, just in case. She sat rhythmically bumping her bare, filthy heels against the rungs of her chair. Although she was moving, she gave an impression of unusual stillness. She seemed hidden, even though she was sitting right there. Her nose and lips were small and finely drawn. Her large eyes were receptive and guarded at once. Her features were pretty, but there was something crumpled, almost collapsed, in her. At the same time, she had something that was very erect and watchful, something that didn't yet show on her face. She sneezed into her hand and reached into the back pocket of her torn jeans for a wadded tissue, which she vigorously dug into both nostrils, then returned to her pocket. She sniffed daintily. She hadn't bathed for a while and she smelled bad, but she didn't know it.

Elise was sixteen, and she had run away from home. She had come from Marin County to Vancouver. She had been getting money by begging on the street, and while she always got enough to buy the fried food and packaged snacks that she liked, she wanted to find a job. It was hard because she didn't have any papers that said she was a Canadian of legal age. People said those papers were easy to fake, but so far she hadn't figured out how.

She had gotten across the border by hitching a ride with two men who were taking horses to Vancouver for a big horse show. They had hidden her in the back of the van with their horses. The older of the two was fat and English, and the younger was slim and wiry, with bitterness and happiness wound together in his own special shape. They seemed pleased that she was hitchhiking. They seemed to think it was very funny.

'Doesn't she remind you of one of those silent-movie stars?' said the younger one. 'Sort of passive and ephemeral?'

The older guy glanced at her with a luxuriant turn of his thick neck. 'Yeah,' he said, 'she's like that.'

They asked her how old she was, and she said eighteen. They said that just before they crossed the border, they'd stop and let her get in back with the horses. If the guards looked in back, they'd say she was there to groom the horses for them. But, they said, she absolutely had to be eighteen, or they could really get in trouble. She promised that she was. But the border guards didn't even look in the back of the truck.

When the men let her out in Canada, they invited her to come eat with them at a diner that had a rotating sign shaped like a halfmoon on top of it. The men ate sandwiches filled with meat and mayonnaise and little sliced tomatoes abundantly dripping out. Elise had a strawberry milk shake and a piece of blueberry pie. The men ate with a gusto that almost disgusted her; it made her want to draw back fastidiously, but it also made her want to join in and have gusto too. 'You know,' she said, 'I'm not really eighteen. I'm sixteen.' There was silence. The big English guy stopped eating. Elise loudly sucked up the last of her milk shake.

'Fucking hell,' said the Englishman. 'Fucking little liar.'

'You selfish bitch,' said the young one. 'Do you know how much trouble we could've been in? They'd of held us back and we'd miss the show!' All his happiness was gone, and his bitterness was coming out in a straight line. 'You can just get your stuff out of our truck and get your ass back on the highway,' he said.

They went out to the parking lot, the young man strutting with anger. 'And another thing,' he said. 'When someone stands you a meal, you're supposed to say thank you.' He threw her backpack on the ground.

She walked away so upset she trembled. She didn't understand why they had gotten so mad when they'd thought everything else was so funny. She was a liar and a selfish bitch and rude. But then a woman in a fancy car had stopped to pick her up and Elise had sped away like she didn't have to be those things anymore. She'd been glad she'd lied to those jerks.

A nurse with big white legs and blond hair on her arms came out with a file folder and said, 'Elise?'

Elise followed the nurse back into the examining room. She took off her pants and put on a paper gown, and a woman doctor with a sad, handsome face came in and shook her hand. The doctor talked to her about AIDS and asked her questions about sex. She took blood from her arm and asked her to lie down for a pelvic exam. During the pelvic exam, the doctor asked her if she'd ever seen the inside of her vagina. When she said no, the doctor asked if she wanted to look. The doctor seemed to think it was a good idea, so Elise said okay. She lifted her head and looked in the mirror that the doctor was holding between her legs. The doctor smiled encouragingly. Elise thought that the doctor was doing this because she was trying to encourage Elise to relate to her body in a caring way, so she looked with what she hoped was a caring expression. It was a rather startling sight, probably because of the metal thing. 'Thank you,' she said. Fleetingly, she thought of the men with the horses and how they'd feel if they could see how polite she really was.

When she went back out into the waiting room, a group of people were clustered about the receptionist's desk, so she had to wait a moment to make another appointment. As she stood there, she looked again at the support group flyers on the bulletin board. A small piece of torn-out notepaper with pink writing and drawings of flowers and a cat caught her attention. 'Baby-sitter needed,' it said. 'Good pay, friendly environment. No phone. Apply in person.' Elise recognized the street address; it was near Pigeon Park, only a few blocks from where she was staying. She asked the receptionist how long the ad had been there.

'Baby-sitting?' The woman looked up, alarmed. She had a tiny green tear tattooed under one dark eye. She got up and went to the bulletin board. 'Who put *that* there?' she demanded. She tore the ad off the board, crumpling the flowers and the little cat into a ball. 'That shouldn't even be here,' she said.

But Elise remembered the address, and she went there straight from the clinic. The address was a tenement building in a slum with a dull, vaguely benevolent character. A family of foreigners sat on the front steps, drinking and spreading their lives out for anyone to see. The father sat holding a beer can between his big knees. He was sweating through his undershirt. There were patches of black hair on his fatty upper arms. He seemed intensely aware of Elise, even though he looked away. Inside, the foyer was close and full of innocuous smells made big and nasty by the heat. The glass in the door had been shot at and taped up. Elise pushed a dirty little button and a woman's voice came furrily through the intercom. She had to come down to let Elise in.

She was very small and thin, and she seemed to flicker in the dark hall. Even from a distance, her personality shot off her body. When she opened the splintered door, her smile was tremulous and tight. She was about twenty-five. She made Elise think of a small, bright fish darting through deep water.

'I'm Robin,' she said as they walked up the stairs. 'I'm so glad to see you. I couldn't afford to run an ad in the papers, and I wasn't sure who would see the ones I put up.' Her voice was light and excited; it pulled on Elise with the tactile intelligence of a small child who wants something. 'You're exactly the kind of person I was hoping for, thank God.' She rounded a corner and looked back at Elise, her eyes wide and one hand on her heart.

The apartment was a large room. There was a sink and a hot plate and a furiously humming refrigerator. The bathroom door was open; it looked like it was the size of a closet. Two little boys, about six and four, looked at Elise, the younger one peeping from behind his brother. There was an infant lying on the king-size bed in a diaper, softly jerking its limbs with the private movement of its thoughts. Robin offered Elise a chair with a vinyl seat and sat on the bed.

'You see the situation,' she said. She looked Elise in the eyes, as if acknowledging something she'd prefer not to mention directly. 'We're from Sacramento,' she said. 'And I'm going to tell you the truth. We're here illegally. I just drove us across the border. I said we were shopping and kept going. I had to leave because my husband was abusing me and he was starting to hurt the boys. I couldn't stand it anymore.' She sat very straight, with her legs tautly crossed. 'I was afraid all the time,' she said. 'I didn't want the boys to . . . to . . .' She made a strange crumpled gesture.

There was a silence. The children were in the corner playing with their toys, but Elise felt their attention on their mother.

'I'm an American too,' she said. 'I ran away from home too.'

To her surprise, Robin smiled. 'So we have something in common,' she said. 'Were your parents abusive?'

Elise hesitated. She pictured her father sitting in his armchair, looking miserable.

Robin held up her hand. 'It's okay,' she said. 'You must've had your reasons. You can tell me later if you want, and if not, that's okay.'

Elise said she had done a lot of baby-sitting but hadn't taken care of an infant before. Robin said that it was okay, that she would make up some bottles of formula before she left in the morning. She would show Elise how to change diapers.

'There's one thing, though,' she went on. 'I know it's bad, but I can't pay you for at least a week. I don't even have a job. That's why I need a baby-sitter. I need to find a job. Until then I need every penny for food. I know it's asking a lot. But if you can just stick with me for a few weeks, I promise I'll take care of you.'

'Okay,' said Elise. She felt irritated with herself for saying it; she wasn't sure why she had.

'Thank you,' said Robin. 'I know it sounds flaky, but I'm a good judge of people. I feel I can trust you. Only two other people have come by, and they were just . . .' She gestured with distaste. 'Druggy, crazy. I was getting frantic, you understand.'

Elise nodded. She felt as if Robin had reached out and grabbed her.

Robin asked if she could start the next day at nine o'clock. She said she had a job interview at ten. 'I think I'll be back around three,' she said. 'But if he offers me a job right away, I'll take it. Then I probably won't be back until six or so.'

It did not occur to Elise to ask what kind of job it was, or why the interview was being conducted on Sunday morning. Robin introduced the children. The oldest boy's name was Andy and the little one was Eric. The baby was Penny. The boys looked at Elise gingerly, as if she might do anything.

Elise left feeling strange about the arrangement. She was glad she had a job, but she didn't like having to wait for money. The family on the porch registered her departure. The little girl crouched and stared up at her as if from the bottom of a pit.

She went back to the flat she was sharing with a guy named Mark. She had not known him until four weeks ago. He was the friend of a girl in Seattle named Wren, and when she told him that Wren had given her his address, he let her in. He was a pale, exhausted twenty-five-year-old with an air of affable ruin. He offered her a cup of tea. They sat together in the living room and talked while he sewed leather patches onto his jeans with dental floss. He told her he had come to Vancouver to stop using heroin and to recover from romantic disappointment. He sewed very deliberately, as if each fine, repetitive movement replenished his faith in the bodily truth of his existence. He told Elise that his roommate had gone to London for the summer; she could stay in his room. She had been sleeping there since then. The sour, musty little mattress was covered by a faded flannel sheet with blue sheep on it. Instead of a blanket, there was a heavy pink curtain that she slept under. Once she got used to it, she'd come to like its exaggerated scratchiness.

She found Mark in the kitchen, drinking tea out of a flowered china cup and reading an article about an actress who had been a porn star at the age of twelve. She told him about the baby-sitting job, the abusive husband and the no money at first.

'It sounds fucked up,' said Mark cautiously. His face had the abstract look of someone who has just categorized something and then quickly stepped away from it.

'I think she's just freaked out,' said Elise.

'I guess she would be.' Mark scratched his stomach and blinked at the sunlight trembling on the table.

For some reason, this conversation made her more determined to make the job work. She lay in bed that night, imagining herself going to the apartment every day, playing with the children and caring for them. She imagined greeting Robin as she came home from work with that tremulous smile on her face, her shoulders drooping as she stooped to take off her shoes. They would form a team. Elise would save money. Years later, Robin would still write to her to tell her how the kids were doing. Elise lay awake under the curtain all night, thinking these thoughts and listening to people walk up and down outside the window. Every now and then, one of them would yell terrible abuse, and she would strain to hear it.

In the morning she had some of Mark's bread and cheese for breakfast, along with olives snuck from an old jar, and left to baby-sit. There were only a few people on the street; they seemed random yet deeply set in their private purposes. Two men with big blunt faces walked along drinking beers and talking about how some ridiculous awful thing that was always happening had happened again. 'Pop goes the weasel!' said one. 'Yeah, pop goes the weasel,' said the other. A pretty, peevish young man in a dress and a wig swiftly padded along in his stockinged feet, his tiger-striped pumps and matching purse in one hand. A middle-aged woman carrying three heavy bags pressed forward as if she had decided that no other direction was allowed.

The front porch of Robin's apartment building was bare except for a child's red plastic bucket with some dirty water and a dead goldfish in it. Robin let her in, greeting her as if they were both already far away in some happy future. The two boys, however, were sitting at a rickety table eating bowls of cereal, and the baby was sitting up on the bed, flailing its tiny fists at the present. The older boy, Andy, stopped his spoon in midair and watched her. His eyes made her feel guilty, even though it wasn't her fault.

'Penny's just dropped a load,' said Robin, 'so I can show you how to change her.'

They sat on the bed, and Robin laid the infant on her back, supporting her head with one slim, splayed hand. She unfolded the diaper as if it were a little paper puzzle. The smell of perfect shit rose into the air. The baby's private body was blank as the flesh of a plant. She kicked her legs, working the fierce new engine of her body. Robin's hands were deft and quick, and Elise thought their movements pleased the baby. Elise expected that Robin would want her to redo the diaper, to show that she had learned, but instead Robin just smiled and said, 'See?' The baby gurgled at her mother's big smile. Robin showed her the bottles of formula she had prepared and told her how to heat them. Then she opened a badly dented tin cupboard and showed her a jar of peanut butter, some bread, and a yellowing orange that they could eat for lunch.

'I know you'll do great,' said Robin. She turned to the boys; her smiling profile tingled wildly. 'Be good for Lisa,' she said.

When she left, the air felt roiled, like water in the wake of a furious propeller. Elise sat on the bed. The boys sat at the table with their eyes down. Eric, the little one, fiddled with his spoon as if he were rubbing a secret comfort spot. Elise looked at the baby; it dispassionately stared back. She looked at the boys. She had lied about her baby-sitting credentials; she had had very little experience with children. She went and sat at the table with them.

'Hi,' she said.

She felt something move between the brothers, invisible and cellular. Andy looked up and back down. Eric watched him.

'Do you like animals?' she asked.

'Um hm,' said Andy. His brown eyes showed intelligence and strength, veiled by a thin, protective opacity.

'We have a cat,' she said. 'His name is Blue.'

'We have a dog at home,' said Andy.

Eric looked up suddenly and said, 'His name is Roscoe.'

'He's a genius,' said Andy. 'For a dog.'

They both looked at her. Eric had a delicate elfin chin. His intelligence seemed more fragile than his brother's.

'Blue was an orphan when we found him,' she said. 'He was living with his brothers and sisters under a deserted house.'

'What's an orphan?' asked Andy.

'Children with no parents. The mother cat had left them, and my brother Rick found them when his friend's dog ran up to the house and started barking because he smelled cats. Blue was just four weeks old, but he came out and stood up to the dog. He arched his back and spat, and the dog was so surprised he just stopped. Rick saved the litter and we adopted Blue.'

She expected them to cheer Blue, or to ask about him, but instead they abruptly slid off their chairs and ran to play with their toys. She was puzzled and even a little hurt; she thought they would like the story. She walked over to where they played and crouched beside them. They had a strange assortment of toys, some of which weren't even toys. They had rubber dinosaurs, colored rocks, a metal truck, a turtle with hair, a cymbal with a pink elastic wrist strap, a stuffed dog, a battery-operated gorilla, a knotted leather cord with two marble balls on either end, a wind-up chickie, and a ceramic mermaid. Alex had the metal wind-up chickie and Eric had the mermaid. They talked urgently in cartoon voices and marched their toys around so that they acted out a story. They talked loudly, as if they were putting on a show for her and, at the same time, using their loudness to shut her out. On impulse, she picked up the gorilla and made it walk up to Eric's mermaid. 'Hey, good-lookin',' she said. Eric tensed. 'Hey,' she said. She wiggled the gorilla. Eric ignored her; she blushed. She felt as if she were trying to squeeze into a spot too small for her. She decided to do the dishes, even though there were only two of them.

She washed the cereal bowls with a little bit of green steel wool. Then she wiped the counter with it. She looked at the baby, who wasn't doing anything. She sat at the table by the window. On the table was an old digital clock and an empty bud vase made of clouded plastic. The clock said 9:41. Elise looked out the window. There were people out walking around now, and she watched them. Normally at this time of day she would be walking up and down Granville, asking people for change. Most of the panhandlers her age sat on the sidewalk and begged in groups. They sat huddled as if they were glad to have arrived at the absolute bottom, where it was nice and solid and they could sit. They sat huddled as if protecting something very special, and their begging seemed like an afterthought. Elise much preferred the walking method. People were more apt to give you money if you went up to them and asked them for it, and besides, she liked the big dumb rhythm of everybody going in the same two directions and, inside that, all the tiny, concentrated rhythms of different walking styles. She liked moving quickly in and out of other people's rhythms.

Sometimes she'd have a conversation with someone who gave her money or insulted her, and for a moment that person would loom out of the generality with a loud blare of specificity and then fade back as Elise walked on. Once, she had approached a young guy who had come out of a fast food store and was opening the box of fried chicken he'd bought there. He gave her a dollar. He said he was giving it to her because she reminded him of a girl he knew in San Francisco. 'She's a sex worker,' he said, 'a pros-tee-tute.' He dragged the word out singsong style and smiled at her with an aggressive, bristling air as rank and particular as a deep body smell. 'I've thought of doing that,' she said. His aggression turned into surprise and then into a funny, sour acceptance. He asked her if she wanted some chicken. She said yes and tore all the fried juicy skin off the breast. 'Hey,' he said, 'it's no good without the skin,' but he still let her sit with him and eat, even though she'd ruined his chicken.

Andy ran over to her with his metal chickie. 'This is Jago,' he said. 'He's a fighter orphan bird. When the hunters come into the forest to get birds and they see Jago, they scream and run away!'

'Oh!' said Elise.

'You pretend to be the hunter,' said Andy. 'You're coming in the woods and you see this bird and you don't know it's Jago so you start to shoot, okay?'

Elise pretended that her finger was a gun and pointed it at the metal chick.

Andy flipped up one of the chick's metal wings to reveal *Jago* written on the underside in felt pen.

Elise waited.

'It's Jago!' prompted Andy.

'Oh, no!' said Elise. 'Jago!'

Andy ran back to his game in triumph.

Little kids always wanted to set things up so they got to yell a certain satisfying thing or to make you yell it. When she was little, she or her brother Rick would yell something like, 'Why did Miss Grinch and Miss Butt take all their clothes off?' and the other would yell back, 'Because they wanted to!' Then they would roll around, tickling each other and giggling, yelling more questions and yelling the same answer again and again.

The sunlight shifted, and the surface of the table became warm and bright. Elise extended her arms into the warmth; her pale arm hairs stood up in the air, and the sight made her feel tender toward herself. All those thousands of tiny hair follicles, each earnestly keeping its special hair going. She lifted her arm and rubbed the soft hairs against her lip. Outside, a child flashed down the street, waving something bright in his hand.

When she was seven and Rick was eight, they would dress in skirts and hats and dance around the mulberry bush in the backyard of their old house, picking the berries and singing, 'Oh, we haven't got a chance for our vegetables! For our vegetables!' Their mother had taken pictures of them in their outfits, each holding a plastic bucket of mulberries. Elise stood with her stumpy little legs apart and made her stomach stick out on purpose. Rick posed with one hand on his slim hip, his smile innocent and arrogant and glad. His bare legs were long and finely shaped and made him look more delicate than he was.

With a soft blending motion, that memory turned into another one. She and Rick cuddled on the couch while the family watched TV. Their mother sat on the end of the couch with her legs tucked up under her; Rick leaned against her hip and Elise sat against him. They were eating sticky refrigerator cookies and watching *It's a Wonderful Life*. Through her thin nightgown she could feel his warm haunch and his bare foot, cool and faintly sweaty against her thigh. He was radiant, thoughtless, quick, and very male. His heart was tender, but the rest of him was darting around too fast for him to feel it. Elise could feel it, though. Their mother's old knit afghan covered their laps and legs, and while their heads were busy watching TV and eating the special cookies, under the afghan she was knowing him and letting him know her, in an invisible way too complicated for words. Meanwhile, their father presided in his leatherette recliner. Their little brother, Robbie, sat close to the TV, but instead of watching the movie, he was concentrating on his red crayons and his drawing. They were safe in their lair.

It was very hot in the apartment, hotter than outside. She was already sweating around the waistband. She glanced at the boys; she wished she could take off her shirt but she wasn't sure it was right, even though it was natural.

In Seattle, she had stayed for a few weeks in an apartment with ten other kids. It was okay to take off your shirt or change your clothes there, whether or not you were having sex with anyone. She'd had sex with a boy named David who stayed there sometimes. Even before that they saw each other naked sometimes because they liked each other so much, like brother and sister. He had green eyes with black eyelashes, and a wine-colored birthmark on his prominent right hipbone. He had written a whole page in his journal about her and then read it to her. But the day after they slept together, he took acid and went off with some other guys to steal animal statuary, and she never saw him again. It was all right; she understood that they were both traveling. But she wished she had an address where she could write to him.

'No! No! No!' Eric's whine was smothered and aggrieved. Elise sat up and listened alertly to see if Andy was picking on him. 'Okay,' said Andy. 'Now they're going to attack the mall.' 'Okay,' said Eric. Elise relaxed.

Rick had picked on Robbie a lot when they were little. Before their parents got divorced, he picked on him just by laughing at him. Then the divorce happened. The children went to live with their mother, even though she couldn't afford them. Everybody was upset and unhappy. Their mother cried all the time. Elise had bad dreams. Robbie wet the bed. Rick began hurting Robbie. He slammed the car door on his leg. He punched him in the stomach while he was asleep. He peed on his drawings.

Their mother would yell and then she'd cry, and for a while Rick would try to be nice to Robbie. He would put his arm around his little brother and share his ice cream cone and smile like they were in a secret league together. There would be two feelings in his eyes when he did this. One of the feelings was mocking, as if his kindness was just another, more complicated version of his meanness. But the other feeling was pure sweetness for Robbie. It was so sweet Rick couldn't resist feeling it, and so sweet that he couldn't quite stand feeling it. So he would just taste it, like a piece of candy, and then throw it away. But Robbie couldn't help reaching out for the sweetness. He would look up at Rick and then look down and reach for the ice cream cone and politely eat at it with the shy tip of his tongue. Rick would look at him, and tenderness would shimmer under his eyes, trying to get out. But then he would go back to being mean again.

Their mother would yell when Rick was mean, but she loved him too much to really punish him. She loved his boyish arrogance and his radiance. When he bragged about winning in sports or outsmarting somebody or even being mean, she would look at him as if he had something she needed more than anything in the world. And he would bathe in her look. She would come up behind him and stroke his hair, and he would act like he wasn't paying attention, but really he would lean into his mother, welcoming her. She would ask him to do things: open a can, carry a bag of groceries, kill a big bug, rub her feet with oil. And he would do it with an air of chivalry, even though she was the bigger and stronger one. Maybe their mother had been afraid that if she lost the meanness, she'd lose the chivalry, and she couldn't bear to lose that. But she loved Robbie too, and she was frightened by the way Rick treated him.

So she got cheap state psychiatrists to look at Rick and Robbie. Once a week they would go to a clinic to be examined, while Elise sat in the waiting room with her mother. Elise didn't mind going to the clinic. She kind of liked sitting on the orange furniture in the lounge, eating candy out of the machine at the end of the hall and observing the mentally ill people who went in and out. She liked her mother's certainty that, finally, she was accomplishing something.

But the psychiatrists didn't find anything wrong, and things went back to normal. Then Rick hung Robbie upside down in a neighbor's barn and made him swing back and forth until Robbie's head hit the wall and his forehead cracked open. When their mother saw, she screamed and put her hand over her mouth; then she turned and hit Rick in the face. She bundled Robbie up and carried him to the house, his forehead bleeding onto her pink blouse, one leg hanging limp off to the side. She didn't cry; she made choking, struggling noises that were terrible and female. Elise ran after her; Rick just stood there.

That night Elise had a dream about Robbie. She was in the fifth grade, and had just learned about how Mount Vesuvius had erupted. In her dream, a volcano had erupted in San Anselmo, and their father came in the car to save them. While they were driving to safety, Elise looked back and saw that they had forgotten Robbie. He was running after the car, screaming for their father to stop. Elise held her hand out the window for him to grab, but their father wouldn't slow down.

Her dream came true, sort of. Their father married a woman who owned and operated a salon where she tattooed color onto women's faces so that they would look like they had makeup on all the time. It was decided that Rick and Elise should go live with their father and his new wife and her daughter, Becky, while Robbie stayed behind with their mother. It wasn't until years later that it had occurred to Elise that the barn incident had something to do with this arrangement.

'I'm cutting his head off! I'm cutting his head off!' yelled Andy.

'No!' Eric's voice had a shrill, stubborn push.

Swiftly, Elise crossed the room. 'Don't cut off his head!' she said.

There was a burst of silence. Elise felt the boys shrink deeper into their privacy. Stiffly, they moved their toys. She felt embarrassed. She thought of saying, 'Be nice to Eric,' but she was too embarrassed. She stood over them, feeling she couldn't move until something else happened.

'What are you playing?' she asked.

Andy looked up. 'The turtle is trying to cut off the

mermaid's friend's head and Jago is coming to help,' he explained patiently.

'Oh.' She relaxed. They relaxed. She stood there a minute in the new atmosphere. Then she went to check on Penny. The baby was still just lying there. Elise sat on the bed, feeling that everything was okay. She had shown authority and made contact. She thought about picking the baby up and walking back and forth with her, but she'd never picked a baby up before. Instead, she put her hand on Penny's stomach and rubbed her. The baby smiled and made sounds that were like light, tumbling bubbles. Nervously, Elise stroked the exquisite little forehead. The baby looked at Elise solemnly and then drew her gaze back inward as she returned to the business of creating a person who could survive in the world. Elise looked out the window. Two shabby old women wearing brimmed hats stood on the pavement, talking. They touched each other and smiled and nodded vigorously.

It was funny, thought Elise, that she had told the children 'we have a cat' when she wasn't with her family anymore. He wasn't her cat now. They hadn't discovered Blue under a porch with an orphaned litter, either. And he had never faced down a dog. He was an expensive Persian cat from a breeder. Their father had bought him as a special gift for their stepmother, Sandy.

When she and Rick moved in with their father and Sandy, their father had said to her, 'Now you'll have a sister,' as if she had always wanted one. But she had not wanted, at the age of eleven, to have a nine-year-old stranger dropped into the middle of her life. It was like suddenly having to live with somebody who sat across the room from her at school.

But Becky was nice. She was diffident and she always shared. She was also weird, or, as her own mother said, 'neurotic.' She picked the fur off her stuffed animals. All her animals were bald. Her mother said it was because she needed to 'act out her anger' at her parents' divorce. It didn't look like anger to Elise. Becky would sit with an animal and suck her thumb and pick the fur off it with two fingers, collecting it in her palm until she had a handful. Then she'd put it in a blue plastic bucket called 'the picky bucket.' If you wanted to torture Becky, and Rick and Elise sometimes did, you could threaten to dump the pickies in the toilet or throw handfuls about the room while Becky screamed and ran around trying to catch them. Even when she got older and stopped picking the animals, Becky kept the overflowing picky bucket under her bed. Then her mother found them and threw them away, because she said it was 'over the top' for Becky to have them. For a while after that, Becky defiantly picked the stuffing out of the mattress and dropped it on the floor, but she was really too old by then, so she didn't do it long.

Elise came to like Becky and to feel protective of her shy peculiarity. But she was more impressed by her stepmother. Rick had hated Sandy from the beginning, but Elise found her too strange and fascinating to hate. Sandy was a little younger than their mother, but she had a bright, bristling competence that made her seem older. She was thin and her stomach was hard and she'd had her face tattooed so that she appeared to be wearing full makeup all the time. Even when she got up in the morning, her lips were bright red, her cheeks were pink, and her eyes were outlined in black. 'I fixed it so I wouldn't have to wash my face off at night,' she said. She said it with brisk self-deprecation, as if her face, everybody's face, was a vaguely ridiculous thing that could come off at any moment. She also said it with pride that she'd acknowledged the problem and then gone right in there to fix it. Her whole being seemed to be bursting with self-deprecation and pride and the need to fix things.

Their father may have gotten Blue as a present for Sandy, but he had grown to like the cat more than anybody did. He thought it was soulful and beautiful. He brought Blue special treats and talked to him, even sang to him. Blue would be resting on the floor, and their father would bend over to look the cat in the face and he would sing: 'Six foot, seven foot, eight foot – bunch! Daylight come and Blue wants to go home!'

Rick despised it when their father did that, and would imitate him viciously. Elise defended their father and reminded Rick that he had been in Vietnam, where he'd risked his life and fought.

'Yeah,' said Rick. 'The retards are strong.'

This was the thing he said when somebody who was ugly or unpopular did something smart. He could say that and take anything away from anybody. When she was younger, it hurt her to hear Rick talk about their father this way. But when she got older, she saw what he'd meant; their father was kind of a retard. She remembered him at the dinner table, yelling.

'You think you're such a bunch of smart, tough feminists!' he yelled. 'But you don't know anything! About men, about sex!' He grabbed the edge of the table and lunged over his dish. 'There's guys out there who would cut your bowels out to have it!'

Elise looked at Rick and rolled her eyes. Becky, who was fourteen, began to cry. 'See!' said their father. 'The big feminist! Crying!' But his voice wobbled on the second exclamation, as if it was embarrassed, and his last word was almost sorry about the whole thing. He withdrew into his chair, wiped his mouth, and ate with the slightly offended air of someone who just wants to mind his own business.

Because They Wanted To

If Sandy had been there, he would never have said those things. But she was at a codependency meeting, which was why he was in a bad mood to begin with.

Elise looked at Becky so she would see that Elise didn't look down on her for crying, but Becky was busy composing herself and didn't notice. Elise was angry and disgusted that their father had made Becky cry when he had actually been yelling at Elise for talking about a woman on TV who'd been saying that if girls wanted to dress like prostitutes, they should learn to act like prostitutes. Becky sniffed, tucked her fine red hair behind her ears, and took up her silverware with the delicate resolve of a young cat. Elise furtively tried to meet her brother's eye so he would see how contemptuous she felt, but Rick was too deep in his own special contempt to respond. He stroked his dyed black hair and fidgeted disdainfully as if trying to locate some small spot worth being in, even though he knew such a spot didn't exist, at least not among *these people*. One cuff of his angora sweater slid down over one long, severely articulated hand, adding to the exquisite quality of his disdain. Elise felt a pang of admiration for him. She felt dejected that he wouldn't look at her, but she didn't blame him. He was seventeen, and not necessarily interested in looks across the dining table, and anyway, if she were as beautiful as Rick, she thought, she'd be stuck-up too.

The next day Elise was watching TV with Becky and Rick when their father walked through the room in a state of mild, enchanted absence. He looked as if he were in a private landscape, a place of secret relief only he knew about. He passed Becky, and as he did, he reached out and, with one finger, playfully stroked the bridge of her nose and said, 'Ski nose! Ski nose!' She giggled and forgave him. He patted her shoulder and moved on. Elise had boiled with anger.

Andy and Eric ran around the room, happily screaming. Andy waved the knotted leather cord and banged the marble balls together. Eric beat the cymbal with a colored rock. Their energy unspooled crazily and spilled all over the room. Andy ran up to Elise like a kitten dancing around a cat. He held up the banging balls and gave a shrill little scream and hopped around. Eric looked on. Elise smiled uncertainly. She wanted to answer their excitement, but she felt too big and stiff. She couldn't remember that kind of excitement and was tentative and vulnerable before it. The boys ran to the bed and chased each other around it, yelling and banging. Elise remembered jumping up and down on the mattress with Rick, yelling, 'Because they wanted to!' The boys pounced on the bed and rolled around, tickling. A little strip of feeling wiggled free inside her. She burst off the chair and jumped on the bed, grabbing Andy and tickling him. He squealed and turned in to her embrace with a shy, writhing twist. Penny began to scream. Everything closed up.

'Stop it,' said Elise. She sat up and pried Andy off her. 'Be quiet now.'

The boys looked down nervously. Elise put her hand on Penny and made her rock on the squishy mattress. The baby kept screaming. Elise felt a hard little hiccup of fear. The boys slid off the bed and went away. Her fear got bigger. Frightened, she slid her hands under the baby and took it in her arms. Penny bellowed and wet through her diaper. Elise didn't know what to do. She didn't remember how to change the diaper. She walked the length of the floor with the baby, turned and walked the other way. Her heart pounded. Maybe Penny would stop screaming before the pee got sticky and itchy. Then Elise could think about the diaper. She tried to walk slow and soothingly.

Sometimes her father would run around and scream because the dog down the street wouldn't stop barking. For a while, she would come home from school every day and would find her father yelling about the dog and her stepmother pretending not to hear him. Elise would go upstairs and knock on Rick's door, and he would let her in, putting on a show of reluctance but smiling. 'Hi, Leesy,' he would say. He would sit on the bed and play his guitar, hunching in on himself as he sang her a song. Or they would sit on his orange pile rug, eating candy corn left over from Halloween and making fun of their father for going crazy over the dog.

'I'm going to kill him!' screamed their father. 'I'll beat his skull in!' There was yelling and scuffling, and then the back door slammed.

'Yeah, right,' said Rick.

But when the dog stopped barking, they were fascinated and nonplussed. If their father had beaten the neighbor's dog to death, what would happen next? 'They'd put him in jail,' said Elise.

'Nah,' said Rick. 'Just a fine, but it would embarrass him.'

They filed down the stairs in excited apprehension. Elise looked back at Rick; he put his hands over his mouth and bugged out his eyes. He meant to be funny, but with his smirking mouth covered, his distended eyes had the flat hysteria of a mask.

'If he kills that fucking dog I'll divorce him, and I mean it. I mean it! It's not normal! What kind of person would go after a dog with a golf club?'

'An asshole,' said Rick.

Sandy banged her hand on the counter and yelled, 'Shut up!' Her voice broke; she had hit her hand hard enough to hurt it.

Their father came in the back door. His face wore an

expression of gentle puzzlement, his golf club was dozing in his hand. He looked as if he been holding a baby against his breast. 'That poor sonofabitch is lonely,' he said mildly. 'When he saw me coming, he started jumping up and down, wanting me to play with him. No wonder he barks! They've got the sad bastard on a short leash, walking around in his own shit.' The frilly green curtain on the back window flared out behind his armpit, the little brass bell attached to the curtain rod dangled above his head. Elise thought of the frilled collar and silly hat of a clown. 'I just petted him for a few minutes,' he said. 'And listen, he's still quiet.' He came into the kitchen and put his golf club in a corner. It immediately fell down; he gently muttered 'Shit' and bent to stand it up again, and Elise was stricken with unbearable pity. It hit her so fast, she didn't have time to be furious or contemptuous. She looked at Rick and saw that under his look of bored distaste was a rigid muscular contraction, like a grimace of pain or rage. For a second, it was as if she was seeing through him to his skeleton. Then it was over, and he was Rick again. He was putting Pop-Tarts in the microwave, his long, agile hands moving like they knew nothing about pain or rage.

Her chest sweated from holding Penny against it. The baby's crying had become a steady contemplative grumble, as if she had found an engrossing pocket of misery and was digging around, exploring. The rhythmic little sobs penetrated Elise and attached her to the baby. She sat on the bed and rocked. The attachment was mutual and interlocked. It made Elise feel relaxed; no matter what happened, it would be all right. She thought: formula. Robin had left a bottle of formula on the counter so Elise wouldn't have to heat it again. Still holding Penny, she walked to the counter and got the bottle. Penny took the nipple in her mouth with a neat little grab. She sputtered, panted, then sighed and quieted as she earnestly sucked.

As soon as Penny stopped drinking, she wet herself again. She didn't seem to care, but still Elise thought she'd better try to change her. Carefully she laid the baby on the coverlet. She undid the soaked diaper and took it off. Penny kicked and waved. Elise wet a threadbare washcloth at the kitchen faucet and wiped the baby. Carefully she put a new diaper on. She wasn't sure it was on exactly right, but it would do until Robin got back. She rinsed the washcloth and hung it on a tiny metal rack.

Andy came over. 'We're hungry,' he said. There was a reproachful little push in his voice, and no wonder: it was two o'clock. She got bread and peanut butter and dishes out of the cabinet. The dishes were cheap and bright-colored. There were three cups, two with flowers on them and one with a picture of a hippopotamus carrying a balloon. Elise imagined Robin in the Salvation Army, picking out cheerful dishes; she felt protective allegiance. She stood at the counter, making them all sandwiches. The linoleum on the counter was cracked and faintly buckled. There was moist black mold where the counter met the wall, and a sour smell in the drain. The odorous dirt was lush and dense. It made her feel rooted to the floor and to the making of the food. She thought of her mother, standing at the counter, making food. Mostly she thought of her mother's hips, big and strong and set right against the counter.

She cut each sandwich into four squares and the orange into eight wedges. She poured everybody a cup of milk, and they all sat down to eat. The boys ate with concentrated faces, as if they were exaggerating their satisfaction on purpose, reassuring themselves that it really was good, that there would always be sandwiches and milk for them. Elise remembered the time she and Becky got up before everybody else and made themselves tea and peanut butter sandwiches; it wasn't that good, but they relished the meal because they wanted to. She remembered herself and Rick and Robbie sitting at the breakfast table while their mother hurried around the room in her open coat, fixing pop-up waffles in the toaster. Their mother was always late for work. She poured their little glasses of juice with a quick, jerking motion. She put their plates before them with such force that the food almost slid off. All her movements were like the tail end of a great, bursting effort, like a grab for a lifeline in a midair leap. The children ate breakfast in the center of this surging effort. Unknowingly they aligned with it. They supported their mother with the fierce secret movements of their breath and blood.

If Elise could have written her mother a letter, she would have told her that she remembered how hard she'd worked to get breakfast on the table in the morning and how good her breakfasts were. She would tell her mother she missed her. She would tell her she had a job as a baby-sitter.

Eric looked at her. 'When is our mommy coming?' he asked.

Elise looked at the clock. With a strained click, one white digit became another. It was two-forty. 'She could walk in any minute,' she said, 'but if she doesn't, she'll be back in a few hours.'

Eric looked confused, then disturbed. He licked his finger and picked at the bread crumbs on his plate with it. Andy began a loud singsong chant.

'She'll be home soon,' said Elise. 'Don't worry.'

Andy sang louder and more insistently. He stood up in his chair and thrust his lips in the air like a singing snout. Well, Elise could sing too.

'Six foot, seven foot, eight foot – bunch! Daylight come and Blue wants to go home!'

Andy stopped with his mouth open, his eyes bright and askance. He grinned, jumped off the chair, and sang his crazy noises right at her. He paused.

Elise stood up; she waved her arms and wagged her butt. 'Come Mister Tally Man, tally me banana – daylight come and I want to go home.'

The boys grinned delightedly. Eric gave a high squeak; he darted forward and grabbed her thighs, butting her with his head. She wobbled and sat down, unbalanced and abashed by the sudden burst of feeling. He climbed up on her lap and groped her body like a busy animal. Andy jogged up and down, yodeling triumphantly. Eric planted his knee on her thigh and squeezed her breasts with both hands. That startled her. Boys weren't supposed to do that, but he was only four. She wasn't sure what to do; it seemed mean to make him stop, but if she let him do it, he might think he could do it to anybody and he'd grow up to be the kind of guy who grabs women's boobs on the street. Then Andy came over and grabbed at her too. She sat for a moment, perplexed. If Robin walked in, would she think that Elise was molesting the children? She put her hands on their shoulders and gently pushed. 'Hey,' she said, 'stop it.' They clung stubbornly. She pushed them again, harder. Eric put his face against her and let out an angry, pleading little grunt. The sound shocked her, and she hesitated. Then Andy lost interest anyway. He let go and went off toward his toys. Eric sighed and relaxed against her. Tentatively, she stroked his head. Then she stroked his back.

When she looked at the clock, it was past three. Robin must've gotten her job. Maybe it was a waitress job and they'd hired her on the spot. Elise imagined Robin changing into a soiled, ill-fitting waitress uniform in a dressing closet filled with odd furniture, forgotten sweaters, and a bucket with a dry mop in it. Her small limbs would be bristling with tension and determination. She would smooth the uniform in the depressing mirror and remind herself to smile. She would work frenetically, trying to do too much at once. The manager would yell. She would work through the break, sneaking olives and maraschino cherries from the condiment tray.

Or maybe she hadn't gotten the job. Maybe she had just decided to go for a long walk in the park, eating cheap candy out of a bag. Elise liked to do that. Sometimes when she was finished panhandling, she would take the long walk around Stanley Park, even though she'd been walking all day. It would probably be a treat for Robin to do something like that, after being cooped up in the apartment for days.

But six o'clock came and then six-thirty, and Robin didn't come back. Elise wondered how, if she'd gotten a job, she could know exactly when she'd get home anyway. What if the job had started at three? What if it was a long shift? What if she'd applied for a waitress job and didn't get it, and then looked at the paper and saw one of those 'escort' ads? She pictured Robin in her little summer dress, talking to an escort service man. She pictured Robin sitting and holding her purse with both hands, her knees together and her calves splayed out, one foot tucked behind the leg of her chair.

One night when Elise was begging in San Francisco, a man asked her if she would blow him for twenty dollars. He must've heard her asking other people for money, because she hadn't asked him. She hesitated. She had never blown anybody before. 'Okay,' he said. 'Thirty.' 'Okay,' she said. They had to walk a few blocks to get to his car. She saw that he wore nice pants and shoes. She asked him what he did. 'Never mind,' he said. He had a sour, contracted little face that reminded her of a cat spraying pee on something to mark it. Elise didn't mind the mean expression; there was even something intriguing about it. It looked like it came out of a small, deep spot that was always the same.

When they got in the car he started to drive. 'Are we going back to your place?' asked Elise.

'No,' he said. 'The park.'

For the first time it occurred to her that something bad might happen. She had read in a magazine that according to experts, rapists and killers are less likely to attack people they can identify with on a human level. So she began talking to him about her boyfriend, even though she didn't have a boyfriend. She thought it might remind him of being in love.

'He doesn't like me to do this,' she said. 'But we need the money so much. He's trying to get a band together.'

The man didn't say anything. Light played on his face. He looked like he was alone in the car, thinking about something he didn't like. He drove deep into the park, where there wasn't any light. He stopped the car and took a ten-dollar bill out of his wallet and put it on the dashboard.

'If it's good, you'll get the rest of it,' he said. Then he unzipped his pants and said, 'Go for it.'

Elise hesitated. She felt insulted, and she wasn't sure what to do. She considered telling him that she'd never blown anybody before; it didn't seem like a good idea. She curled her legs up under her, bent, and tucked her hair back. It couldn't be that difficult.

But it was. Her jaw hurt, hairs kept getting down her throat, and it went on and on. Finally he said, 'Oh, Jesus Christ, just hold still and open your mouth.' He grabbed her hair in his fist and furiously worked his hand. There was a horrible taste, and she reflexively spat. He yanked her head up and jerked her over to the other side of the car. Pain tingled across her scalp. She reached for the bill on the dashboard. He swung wildly; he meant to slap her face, but she moved too fast and he just clipped her chin with her fingers. He snatched the bill on the backstroke and crushed it in his hand.

'No,' he said. 'That was shit.' Outraged, he groped between the seats and extracted a packet of Kleenex. He yanked one out with such force that the packet flew into the back seat. He wiped himself furiously. 'You were shit,' he said.

'That's not fair,' she said. Her voice was light and shaky, and her heart patted fast and high in her chest. 'I mean, you got off.' Her voice was still light, but now it was stubborn too.

He paused in his wiping and half turned. The air between them went into a slow, palpable twist. 'You little cunt,' he said. His voice was very quiet. 'I should beat the shit out of you.'

If he grabbed her, she would poke out his eye. She would kick and bite and scratch. Her mind sped up and ran too quickly for her to hear it. She waited.

He threw the bill at her. 'Get out,' he said.

As she walked, her mind stopped racing and she began to think. She didn't know where she was going, but she felt heady and feverish with clarity. She would not be frightened. She would be all right. It was so cold her teeth chattered, but that was all right. She walked a long time. Sometimes she heard voices, and she knew she was passing near groups of people who couldn't hear her. She felt safe and private in the dark.

She emerged on Haight Street. A caravan of street people were arrayed across the edge of the park. She could see them huddled in ragged groups, their belongings on the ground in bundles. Some people walked between groups with a feisty, rakish air. Dogs trotted about, wagging their tails and sniffing people. The scene had a muddy, pushed-down feeling, but inside that was something raw, volatile, and potent as electricity; it could go in any direction, and it was hard to tell which it would be. She walked by a bright-yellow shirt that had been used to wipe somebody's butt. She realized she was trembling.

'Hi.' A woman wearing a purple jacket walked up to her. 'Do you need anything?'

'What?'

'Like condoms or . . . anything?' The woman had a nervous little face and funny-looking glasses. Her jacket had 'Youth Outreach' written on it. 'Um, alcohol pads, bleach, a toothbrush? A cookie?'

'No, thank you,' Elise had said.

It was getting dark. Through the screen, Elise could feel that the air had cooled, but the apartment was still very hot. It was seven-thirty. Andy and Eric were yelling at each other. In a minute, they would start hitting. Elise felt anger come up in her and then go back down.

'Come on,' she said. 'It's time for dinner.'

Andy threw his toy truck on the floor so hard it dented the wood. 'When is Mommy coming?'

'Soon,' she snapped. Except that she didn't realize she had snapped.

Andy and Eric kept fighting at the table, until Andy kicked his brother and Elise yelled 'Stop it!' as loud as she could. Then they sulked. This time, they didn't eat as if they wanted to like the food. They seemed disappointed in it. Elise was sorry she didn't have anything better to feed them, and she was also irritated at having to eat peanut butter again herself. She would rather have had pie or candy bars, and if she had gone out panhandling, she would've been able to. She hoped Robin was working for an escort service, because then she'd bring home enough cash to give Elise some.

After dinner, she heated the formula and fed Penny. The baby was sleepy and docile. She was very wet again, but she wasn't complaining, so Elise didn't change her. She had agreed to stay only until six anyway; Robin could change her when she got home. Penny released the nipple of her bottle with a guttural chirp; a sparkling thread of spit spanned nipple and lip, then broke and fell down Penny's chin. Elise patted it dry with a Kleenex. She put her hand on the baby's stomach and rocked her.

She thought Robin must sleep in this bed with Penny, curled round her protectively as you would sleep with a kitten. Eric and Andy must sleep with them too. The bed was big, but still they would have to sleep close. She wondered if they wore pajamas. That would be uncomfortable in the heat, but it might be even more uncomfortable to touch sticky naked limbs. She pictured them all lying together, the children asleep and Robin awake and blinking in an oscillating band of street light. She wondered if Robin had a light, lacy gown to wear, or a nylon shortie.

Fleetingly, she thought of her mother in the short cotton gowns she called 'nighties.' She wore them with a white rayon peignoir that she had bought when she was eighteen. Elise remembered her mother's short, thick calves, the little hood of fat covering each round knee. Her mother's legs were middle-aged and ugly, but there was something childish and sweet about them.

Every summer Elise went to stay with her mother. She lived with a man who had custody of two sons from a previous marriage because their mother spent so much time in mental hospitals. Elise liked the man and the sons okay. Robbie had turned into a strange, fat kid who read philosophy books that were beyond his age range, but she liked him too. She spent her summer days sleeping late, making blender drinks, and staying out late with her friends. She would come in after midnight and find her mother sitting in the warm dark, watching a late-night talk show in her peignoir and a nightie. Her mother would turn her head to greet Elise. It was too dark to see her expression, but Elise saw in her profile a mix of love and sadness, of gratitude to see her daughter arrive home safely and forlorn bewilderment at the way everything had turned out. The expression repelled Elise and then drew her in. She would go into the kitchen and make them both hot chocolate. They would sit at opposite ends of the couch, drinking cocoa and commenting about the people on the talk show. They showed off for each other, trying to be smart. Elise's repulsion would slowly dissolve into deep comfort, becoming part of and affecting the texture of the comfort.

When the talk show was over, her mother got up and turned on the light and came to kiss Elise good night. Her peignoir would open slightly as she bent into the kiss, showing her neck and sun-reddened upper chest. The diaphanous yoke of her gown was embroidered with small, plain flowers bearing four round petals apiece. Elise imagined how much her mother must've liked the peignoir when she bought it. She imagined her putting it on for the first time, her shy vanity at the way it looked with her skin and chestnut hair. Her mother had been beautiful, and her beauty still whispered in her eyes and skin. When she wore the peignoir, her whispered beauty aligned itself with the coarse redness of her middle age and made it better than beautiful.

A breeze came into the room and dispersed the heat. There was a burst of fractious traffic noise, people honking and playing their radios loud. Someone screamed at someone else that he was a moron, a jerk-off, a spastic freak. Under the light across the street, a girl Elise's age was walking in a short, filmy dress that played about her slim legs. There was a funny strut in her hips and haunches, as if she was very proud and very ashamed at once. She turned around to smile at someone behind her, and the light caught her teasing eyes and dark, shoulder-length hair in motion about her face.

Elise wondered how her mother would react if she knew about the man in the park. She couldn't picture any reaction. She could only envision her mother sitting on the couch, waiting for her daughter with that stoic look of love and sadness. It was a look that was already hurt too much to be surprised by the man in the park, a look that even anticipated him. It was the shadow of the way she used to look at Rick.

Elise thought of her father. She imagined him walking around the house with his fists balled, yelling that the world was a shit pot and his daughter was a whore. But that image quickly dissolved to an image of him sitting alone on the edge of his bed with his head in his hands. She imagined him feeling the way she felt when she had walked through the park alone. He would feel shocked and scared and angry. But he would hold on. Inside, he would have a hard little rock of love for her, and he would hold on to it.

Like an echo of that image, she thought of Robbie, crouching by the TV and doing his drawings while the world threatened to crush him. She thought of Becky, moving through the room with her light-footed, absent grace. She thought of Rick turning away from her, except she only pictured one shoulder and the side of his face, as if he were someone she'd dreamed of and forgotten.

★

It was eight-thirty and dark outside. 'That bitch,' whispered Elise. 'Where is that fucking bitch?'

Andy ran up with a tiny red thing in his hand. 'This is Little Friend!' he said. 'He's in big, big trouble! He's always, always lost!'

'Oh!'

'Hide him!' said Andy. 'You hide him and we'll try to find him!'

She put Little Friend beside one of the kitchen table legs; it took them a surprisingly long time to find it, and when they did, they wanted her to hide it again.

'Put him someplace bad!' they said. 'Someplace scary!'

She put him in the sugar bowl. They looked all over, screaming, 'Little Friend! Little Friend!' until Penny woke and began to mumble irritably.

'Be quiet,' said Elise sharply.

Eric quieted, but Andy kept screaming.

She knelt and grabbed him by the shoulders. 'If you want to play you have to be quiet. Okay?'

He looked at her to see if she meant it. She tried to seem stern, but it was halfhearted and he could tell. As soon as she let go, he began to yell again.

'All right,' she said. 'I don't want to play.' She went and sat by the window. In the window across the street, a woman was standing at a table and folding clothes. Even from a distance Elise could see that she was frowning resentfully. The boys yelled and ran. She ignored them. It was nine-thirty.

At her father's house, Elise had liked to climb on the roof at night. Her father's upstairs den had a sunporch affixed to it, a small, roof-tiled square with a wooden railing that they lovingly called 'the balcony.' One evening she discovered that if she stood on the railing she could get up on the roof, using her sneakers for traction. She climbed right to the top of the house and straddled it, gazing about the neighborhood. She felt very pleased with herself; with a slight maneuver, she had made a special pocket hidden in ordinary life.

The roof had a number of peaks and flat surfaces, and she explored them all. She found she could sit comfortably outside Rick's room and look in. She could see part of Becky's room, and she could look right into the bathroom. Eventually, she grew bold enough to spy on her family. This gave her a strange pleasure she could not have explained. She could see Becky walking around the room listening to music, not dancing or singing but just pacing with an intent, furiously inturned face. She watched Rick while he wrote a song, crouching on the floor and rocking himself, gazing up with big, rapt eyes as he worked his lips, his pencil poised above the page. She watched her stepmother use the toilet. She watched her father sit on the tub and pare his nails. Seeing these things made her feel closer to her family than she did when she was in the same room with them. It made her like them more.

But they got suspicious when they kept hearing muffled noises overhead, and one night her stepmother went out and saw her on the roof. Then they were all mad at her.

'God,' said Rick. 'What a freak!'

'This is not normal behavior,' said their stepmother. 'This is sick.'

Their father stood and wiped his mouth.

It was ten o'clock. Andy grabbed her arm and yanked it. 'Come on!' he said. 'Hide him again!'

'No,' she said, and she pushed him.

He thrust his little face into the air and sang his nonsense song as loud as he could. Penny began to scream.

Elise stood. 'Stop it,' she said.

'Daylight come, banana wanna go home!'

'Shut up!'

'Daylight come daylight come!'

She slapped him in the face. She slapped him so hard his head snapped around. He shut up. He looked up at her and smiled, tremulously.

'I said stop it,' she said.

He put his thumb in his mouth and went and sat in an armchair in the corner. Eric went and sat with the toys. Elise sat back down. She hoped Penny would stop crying without her having to do anything. It was after ten o'clock. She didn't know what to do. She got up and put an unfinished bottle of formula back on the stove to heat. There wasn't much of it left, she noticed.

Her stepmother loved it when things were sick. Her favorite books were true-life stories about drug-addicted fashion models who died horribly or prep school boys who turned out to be murderers. She loved TV movies about people who seemed okay until they became obsessed with a coworker and wound up killing everyone in the office. She was always saying, 'That's not normal!' in a thrilled, disapproving voice. She could say it about a magazine story that described a jealous wife who stalked her husband's lover so she could make her get on her knees and stick a gun in her mouth. She could say it about Becky sitting in her room and playing the same song over and over again.

She disapproved, but part of her seemed secretly to sympathize with the sickness. It was like she thought everybody had it, and the best you could do was to cover it up, and sometimes it would just come boiling out anyway. Then you had to point at it and condemn it, even though you knew you had it too.

Once, Elise heard her talking to a client about the woman's stepdaughter, who was crazy even though she was on Prozac. Elise had stopped by the salon to borrow some money, and she had to wait because Sandy was tattooing the client's lips. The client's lips were swollen and bleeding from the needle, but she wanted to talk anyway.

'I just feel so bad and so helpless. It turns out she's been cutting herself like that for at least a year. All over her arms and her stomach, with a razor.'

'You know,' Sandy had said, 'there's a whole article on it in *Focus* this month. It's just fascinating. It says they do it to distract themselves from the terrible pain they feel inside.'

Penny didn't want to take the bottle. Elise pushed the nipple against her lips again and again, but she kept turning her head and crying. 'Come on,' Elise whispered, low and angry. 'Shut up, come on.' It wasn't fair, she thought. It was ten-thirty. She didn't know what to do.

She thought of her father yelling at Rick. 'You vain, conceited little prick!' he screamed. 'I'd like to see you out in the trenches with the artillery coming in! What would you do, little prick? Dye your hair?' He crouched over Rick so that he could yell at him better. 'Nobody out there would give a fuck about your hair!'

She slammed the bottle on the little bedside table. She yanked the diaper off the baby. Penny screamed angrily. Elise stopped. She put her hand on Penny's stomach. 'I'm sorry,' she said.

When she had finished the bottle, Penny was quiet. It was eleven o'clock. Elise walked up and down the room. If Robin came home now, Elise was going to yell at her. She went to the dresser and began opening the drawers, starting with the top ones. She saw Robin's nylon underwear, a grubby address book, a rubber band, a button with thread still attached. Eric was looking at her from the floor; when he saw she saw him, he looked away. She found a piece of paper; it was the torn-off half of a form letter asking for money for breast cancer research, with phone numbers and a grocery list written on it in chartreuse ink. There was a ballpoint on the bedside table. She sat on the bed, turned the letter over, and wrote on the back: 'It is 11:00 and I am leaving. You said you would be back at six and you are five hours late. Almost anybody else would've left after two hours late. I took this job for no money and I did everything I said I would do. What you've done is wrong. You have acted like an asshole. I'm sorry to do this, and I hope nothing bad has happened to you. But I have to leave. I am not coming back tomorrow.'

She put it on the table. First she put it down flat, then she stood it up between the clock and the bud vase. She decided to wait just five more minutes. The noise from the street was a cool, soothing mumble. The breeze from the window was almost chilling on her lap. Andy had fallen asleep in the armchair. Eric was moving a toy around and humming softly to himself. She thought about herself in the future. She could only imagine loud music and quickly changing pictures, like an advertisement for something on TV. That was okay; it seemed like fun. She imagined herself having fun, then making money, then going back home and buying everybody presents. She imagined how grateful they'd be.

It was eleven-thirty when she left. Penny was deep in her thoughts. Andy was asleep. Eric was still playing and humming to himself. She crouched beside him to say goodbye. He looked at her with somber eyes. He looked like he'd just recognized her. 'Bye,' he said. She touched his arm; he looked down.

The hall was hot and stuffy. It felt like she was already miles away from the apartment. She padded quickly down the stairs. When she reached the next floor, she saw that the people in the apartment directly under Robin's had left their door wide open. She looked in and saw a group of men sitting in shirt-sleeves around the kitchen table, playing cards. They had big arms and broad, jovial faces. A woman with her back to the door was moving vaguely at the sink. The men laughed and drank as they played. 'Excuse me,' she said.

A man got up and came to the door. His face was pock-marked, with little whiskers in the pocks. 'Yes?' He was foreign, she couldn't tell which kind. He wore a red kerchief around his neck, and his nose was big.

'There's kids in the apartment right above you. I've been taking care of them all day, but now I have to go. I don't know where their mother is. She said she'd be back, but she's not, and now I have to go. Could you be sure they're okay?'

He put his hand on his chin and looked past her as if considering.

The woman glanced past the man at Elise; from her expression, it seemed that Elise made no sense to her.

'One of them's only a baby.'

'Okay,' said the man. He pointed upstairs and nodded. 'I check.'

When she got home, she found Mark sitting in the living room, sewing patches on his jeans. She told him what had happened. 'What do you think I should've done?' she asked. 'Do you think it was okay to leave?'

He shrugged. 'What else could you do? She didn't come back.' He concentrated on his pants, very meticulously working the needle. 'She shouldn't have left you there like that.'

Elise sat on the couch. 'Well, but one of them was a baby.'

'You told the neighbors. They'll be okay.'

'I guess.' She stared at the frayed old carpet. There were tulips on it. She felt grateful to be back in her living room, even though it wasn't really hers. 'The thing is, I don't know what I'm going to do. I can't keep panhandling forever. I have to find work somehow.'

'You'll find something,' said Mark. 'It'll be all right.'

She sat a moment. 'I once blew a guy for money,' she said. 'In San Francisco. It was a nightmare. He said he'd give me fifty bucks, but he only gave me ten, and then he hit me.'

'Yeah?'

'And he tasted funny too. Like there was something wrong with him.'

'Elise, God, you shouldn't let 'em come in your *mouth*.'

'Well, I didn't *want* to; it just happened.'

Mark put down the pants and thought. 'Well,' he said, 'this girl who sells roses in Gas Town has been paying me twenty dollars to clean them for her. Like, take off the thorns and the old petals? If you wanted to help me, I could pay you five dollars. Do you want to do that?'

'Yeah,' she said. 'Okay.' She sniffed. 'Thank you, Mark.'

'It's okay.'

She went into the kitchen and raided the refrigerator. She got olives, cheese, tiny green peppers, and cold white rice from an old Chinese take-out box and put it all on a plate and carried it to her room.

The next day she walked by the apartment building, on the opposite side of the street. There was no one sitting on the porch. She looked up at Robin's window; it was open, as it had been when she left. She pictured Robin coming home and screaming, 'Oh, my babies!' She pictured Andy and Eric at the foreign man's table, eating dishes of ice cream. Then she turned the corner and headed for Granville Street, her rubber dime-store sandals hitting her dirty heels with each fleet step.

PENGUIN ARCHIVE

H. G. Wells *The Time Machine*
M. R. James *The Stalls of Barchester Cathedral*
Jane Austen *The History of England by a Partial, Prejudiced and Ignorant Historian*
Edgar Allan Poe *Hop-Frog*
Virginia Woolf *The New Dress*
Antoine de Saint-Exupéry *Night Flight*
Oscar Wilde *A Poet Can Survive Everything But a Misprint*
George Orwell *Can Socialists be Happy?*
Dorothy Parker *Horsie*
D. H. Lawrence *Odour of Chrysanthemums*
Homer *The Wrath of Achilles*
Emily Brontë *No Coward Soul Is Mine*
Romain Gary *Lady L.*
Charles Dickens *The Chimes*
Dante *Hell*
Georges Simenon *Stan the Killer*
F. Scott Fitzgerald *The Rich Boy*
Katherine Mansfield *A Dill Pickle*
Fyodor Dostoyevsky *The Dream of a Ridiculous Man*

Franz Kafka *A Hunger-Artist*
Leo Tolstoy *Family Happiness*
Karen Blixen *The Dreaming Child*
Federico García Lorca *Cicada!*
Vladimir Nabokov *Revenge*
Albert Camus *A Short Guide to Towns Without a Past*
Muriel Spark *The Driver's Seat*
Carson McCullers *Reflections in a Golden Eye*
Wu Cheng'en *Monkey King Makes Havoc in Heaven*
Friedrich Nietzsche *Ecce Homo*
Laurie Lee *A Moment of War*
Roald Dahl *Lamb to the Slaughter*
Frank O'Connor *The Genius*
James Baldwin *The Fire Next Time*
Hermann Hesse *Strange News from Another Planet*
Gertrude Stein *Paris France*
Seneca *Why I am a Stoic*
Snorri Sturluson *The Prose Edda*
Elizabeth Gaskell *Lois the Witch*
Sei Shōnagon *A Lady in Kyoto*
Yasunari Kawabata *Thousand Cranes*
Jack Kerouac *Tristessa*
Arthur Schnitzler *A Confirmed Bachelor*
Chester Himes *All God's Chillun Got Pride*

Bram Stoker *The Burial of the Rats*
Czesław Miłosz *Rescue*
Hans Christian Andersen *The Emperor's New Clothes*
Bohumil Hrabal *Closely Watched Trains*
Italo Calvino *Under the Jaguar Sun*
Stanislaw Lem *The Seventh Voyage*
Shirley Jackson *The Daemon Lover*
Stefan Zweig *Chess*
Kate Chopin *The Story of an Hour*
Allen Ginsberg *Sunflower Sutra*
Rabindranath Tagore *The Broken Nest*
Søren Kierkegaard *The Seducer's Diary*
Mary Shelley *Transformation*
Nikolai Leskov *Night Owls*
Willa Cather *A Lost Lady*
Emilia Pardo Bazán *The Lady Bandit*
W. B. Yeats *Sailing to Byzantium*
Margaret Cavendish *The Blazing World*
Lafcadio Hearn *Some Japanese Ghosts*
Sarah Orne Jewett *The Country of the Pointed Firs*
Vincent van Gogh *For Art and for Life*
Dylan Thomas *Do Not Go Gentle Into That Good Night*
Mikhail Bulgakov *A Dog's Heart*
Saadat Hasan Manto *The Price of Freedom*

Gérard de Nerval *October Nights*
Rumi *Where Everything is Music*
H. P. Lovecraft *The Shadow Out of Time*
Christina Rossetti *To Read and Dream*
Dambudzo Marechera *The House of Hunger*
Andy Warhol *Beauty*
Maurice Leblanc *The Escape of Arsène Lupin*
Eileen Chang *Jasmine Tea*
Irmgard Keun *After Midnight*
Walter Benjamin *Unpacking My Library*
Epictetus *Whatever is Rational is Tolerable*
Ota Pavel *How I Came to Know Fish*
César Aira *An Episode in the Life of a Landscape Painter*
Hafez *I am a Bird from Paradise*
Clarice Lispector *The Burned Sinner and the Harmonious Angels*
Maryse Condé *Tales from the Heart*
Audre Lorde *Coal*
Mary Gaitskill *Secretary*
Tove Ditlevsen *The Umbrella*
June Jordan *Passion*
Antonio Tabucchi *Requiem*
Alexander Lernet-Holenia *Baron Bagge*
Wang Xiaobo *The Maverick Pig*